Happy Birthday (Altrusa)
25 Successful Years!
Hope there are many more.
Best Wishes
Anne Mather

Dear Reader,

An avid reader of romance novels since early teenage years, I had my first novel accepted and published in 1975.

I enjoy the challenge of creating a powerful hero and independent heroine, and breathing life into their characters...showing how attraction, physical and emotional, between this special man and woman becomes *love*....

Harlequin Presents® holds universal appeal, and I am honored to be a small part of that.

Please join me in congratulating Presents on achieving twenty-five successful years. I extend warmest best wishes for continued publishing prosperity.

With love

Helen Bianchin

Helen Bianchin

P.S. As you read this story, I'm sure you'll recognize my hero and heroine—Dominic Andrea and Francesca Angeletti.... And you'd be right to feel that you've met them before—in my last book, *An Ideal Marriage?*

I became fascinated with Francesca and Dominic when they appeared as minor characters in that book. The chemistry between them was so strong, I felt they deserved their own story....

HELEN BIANCHIN

The Marriage Campaign

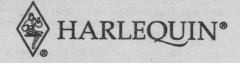

HARLEQUIN®

TORONTO • NEW YORK • LONDON
AMSTERDAM • PARIS • SYDNEY • HAMBURG
STOCKHOLM • ATHENS • TOKYO • MILAN • MADRID
PRAGUE • WARSAW • BUDAPEST • AUCKLAND

ISBN 0-373-11960-7

THE MARRIAGE CAMPAIGN

First North American Publication 1998.

Copyright © 1998 by Helen Bianchin.

This edition published by arrangement with Harlequin Books S.A.

® and TM are trademarks of the publisher. Trademarks indicated with ® are registered in the United States Patent and Trademark Office, the Canadian Trade Marks Office and in other countries.

Printed in U.S.A.

CHAPTER ONE

IT DIDN'T matter how far or how frequent the journey, returning home had a significant effect on her emotions, Francesca mused as the jet banked over the harbour and prepared its descent.

Sydney's cityscape provided a panoramic vista of sparkling blue ocean, numerous coves and inlets, tall city buildings, the distinctive bridge, the Opera House.

Brilliant sunshine held the promise of warm summer temperatures, a direct contrast to those she'd left behind in Rome the day before.

The Boeing lined up the runway and within seconds wheels thudded against the Tarmac, accompanied by the scream of engines thrown into reverse, followed by the slow cruise into an allotted bay.

Collecting baggage and clearing Customs was achieved in minimum time, and Francesca was aware of a few circumspect glances as she made her way through the arrivals lounge.

The deep aqua-coloured trouser suit adorning her tall, slender frame was elegantly cut, her make-up minimal, and she'd caught her dark auburn hair into a loose knot atop her head. The result was an attractive image, but downplayed her status as an international model.

There were no photographers or television cameras in sight as she emerged onto the pavement, nor was there the customary chauffeured limousine waiting at the kerb.

Francesca reached for her sunglasses and slid the dark-lensed frames into place.

She wanted, *needed*, a few days' grace with family and friends before stepping onto the carousel of scheduled modelling assignments, contracted photographic shoots and public appearances.

Cabs formed a swiftly moving queue at the kerb and she quickly hired one, providing the driver with a Double Bay address as he slid out into traffic exiting the international terminal.

Cars, buses, trucks—all bent on individual destinations. Warehouses, tree-lined parks, graffiti decorating—or desecrating, depending on one's opinion—numerous concrete walls. It could be any city in the world, Francesca mused.

Yet it was her city, the place where she'd been born and raised of an Italian immigrant father and an Australian mother who had never quite come to terms with the constraints of marriage.

Francesca retained a vivid recollection of voices raised in bitter recrimination, followed soon after by boarding school, with vacation time spent equally between each parent.

Happy families, she mused with a rueful grimace as she reflected on the years that had followed. Three stepfathers: two who'd bestowed genuine affection and one whose predilection for pubescent girls had become apparent during a school vacation soon after the honeymoon. Acquired step-siblings who had passed briefly in and out of her life. And then, there was Madeline, her father's beautiful blonde wife.

The modelling career which had begun on a whim had succeeded beyond her wildest dreams. Paris, Rome, New York. She had an apartment in each city and was sought after by every major fashion house in Europe.

'Twenty-five dollars.'

The cab-driver's voice intruded, and Francesca delved into her shoulder bag, extracted two notes, and handed them to the driver. 'Keep the change.'

The tip earned her a toothy grin, a business card and the invitation to call him any time she needed a cab.

Francesca slid a coded card into a slot adjacent to double glass doors, and stepped into the lobby as they slid open.

The girl on Reception offered a bright smile. 'Nice to have you back.' She reached beneath the desk for a set of keys and a slim packet of mail. 'The hire car is parked in your usual space. Paperwork's in the glovebox.'

'Thanks.'

Francesca rode the lift to the top floor, deactivated her security system, then entered her apartment.

Beeswax mingled with the scent of fresh flowers. Delicate peach-coloured roses stood in a vase on the sofa table, with a card from her mother. *'Welcome home, darling.'*

A bold display with strelitzia and Australian natives reposed in the middle of the dining room table, with a card from her father, who had inscribed an identical greeting.

The answering machine recorded no less than five messages, and she played them through. A call from her agent; the rest were social. Seven faxes, none of which were urgent, she determined as she flicked through the pages. All, she decided, could wait until she'd had time to shower and unpack. Then she'd go through her mail.

It was good to be home. Satisfying to see familiar things and to know that she would enjoy them for several weeks.

Oriental rugs graced the marble-tiled floor, and there were soft leather sofas in the large lounge area. A formal dining room, modern kitchen, two bedrooms with *en suite* facilities, and floor-to-ceiling glass. Ivory drapes flowed on from ivory silk-covered walls, and the marble tiles were ivory too. Framed prints in muted blue, pink, aqua and lilac graced the walls, the colours accented by several plump cushions placed with strategic precision on sofas and single chairs.

Understated elegance combined with the rich tapestry of individual taste. Lived in, and not just a showcase, she assured herself silently as she took her bags through to the main bedroom.

Unpacking could wait until later, she decided as she stripped off her clothes and entered the *en suite* bathroom.

A leisurely shower did much to ease the strain of too many hours' flight time, and she riffled through her wardrobe, selecting casual cotton trousers and a matching sleeveless blouse, then thrust bare feet into low-heeled sandals.

Collecting shoulder bag and keys, she rode the lift down to the underground car park.

Sydney traffic was swift, but civilised, and far different from the hazardous volume of cacophonous vehicles that hurtled the city streets of Rome.

Italy. The birthplace of her paternal ancestors and the place where she'd met and married world-renowned racing-driver Mario Angeletti three years ago during a photo shoot in Milan, only to weep at his funeral a few months after their wedding when a spectacular crash claimed his life. Last week she'd stood beside an adjacent grave site as her widowed mother-in-law had been laid to rest.

Nothing could be achieved by focusing on the sadness, she rationalised as she drove to the nearest shopping complex.

Her immediate priorities were to access Australian currency and do some food shopping.

Minutes later she parked the car, then crossed to the bank.

There were several people queuing at the automatic teller machine, and she opted for the bank's air-conditioned interior rather than wait in the blazing heat, only to give a resigned sigh at the lengthy column of customers waiting for vacant teller locations.

For a moment she considered saving time by utilising her bank card at the foodhall, then dismissed the idea.

The man in front of her moved two paces forward, and her attention was captured by his cologne. A light, musky exclusive brand that aroused a degree of idle speculation over the man who wore it.

Impressive height, dark, well-groomed hair. Broad shoulders, the muscle structure outlined beneath a fitted polo shirt. Tapered waist, well-cut trousers. Tight butt.

Accountant? Lawyer? Probably neither, she mused. Either would have worn the requisite two-piece suit during office hours.

The queue was dissipating more quickly than she'd anticipated, and she watched as he moved to a vacant teller.

Mid-to-late thirties, Francesca judged as she caught his features in profile. The strong jaw, wide-spaced cheekbones and chiselled mouth indicated a European heritage. Italian, maybe? Or Greek?

The adjoining teller became vacant, and she moved to the window, handed over her access card and keyed in her PIN code, requested an amount in cash, then folded the notes into her wallet.

Francesca turned to leave, and collided with a hard male frame. 'I'm so sorry.' The startled apology tumbled automatically from her lips, and her eyes widened at the steadying clasp of his hand on her elbow.

Dominic's scrutiny was unhurried as it slid negligently down her slim form, then travelled back to linger on the soft curve of her mouth before his eyes lifted to capture hers.

There was something about her that teased his memory. Classical fine-boned features, clear creamy skin that was too pale, gold-flecked brown eyes. But it was the hair that fascinated him. Twisted into a knot at her nape, he wondered at its length. And imagined how it would look flowing loose down her back, its vibrant colour spread out against the bedsheets.

It was an evocative image, and one he banked down.

The breath caught in Francesca's throat at the primitive, almost electric awareness evident, and for endless seconds the room and its occupants faded into obscurity.

Crazy to feel so *absorbed* Francesca decided shakily as she forced herself to breathe normally.

She came into contact with attractive men almost every day of her life. There was nothing special about *this* particular man. Merely sexual chemistry, she rationalised, at its most magnetic.

Recognition was one thing. It was quite another to feel the tug of unbidden response.

She didn't like it, didn't want it.

And he knew. She could see it in the faint curve of that sensually moulded mouth, the slight darkening of those deep, almost black eyes. His smile deepened fractionally, and he inclined his head in silent acknowledgement as he released her arm.

Francesca kept her expression coolly aloof, and with a deliberately careless movement she slipped her wallet into the capacious shoulder bag, then turned with the intention of exiting the bank.

He was a few paces ahead of her, and it was difficult to ignore the animalistic grace of well-honed muscle and sinew. Leashed power and steel. Of body, and mind.

A man most women would find a challenge to explore, mentally as well as physically. To discover if the hinted knowledge in those dark eyes delivered the promise of sensual excitement beyond measure.

Ridiculous, she dismissed, more shaken than she was prepared to admit by the passage of wayward thought. It was merely a figment of an over-active imagination, stimulated by the effects of a long flight and the need to adjust to a different time-zone.

There was a slight tilt to her chin as she emerged onto the pavement. The sun was bright, and she lowered her sunglasses from their position atop her head, glad of the darkened lenses.

Head high, eyes front, faint smile, practised walk. Automatic reflex, she mused as she crossed the mall.

The foodhall was busy, and she took care selecting fresh fruit before adding a few groceries to the trolley. With various family members and friends to see, breakfast was likely to be the only consistent meal she'd eat in her apartment.

Family. A timely reminder that she should make the first of several calls, she determined wryly as she selected milk from the refrigerated section, added yoghurt and followed it with brie, her favourite cheese.

'No vices?' Low-pitched, male, the faintly accented drawl held a degree of mocking amusement.

Francesca was familiar with every ploy. And adept at dealing with them all. She turned slowly, and the light, dismissive words froze momentarily in her throat as she recognised the compelling dark-haired man she'd bumped into at the bank.

He possessed a fascinating mouth, white, even teeth, and a smile that would drive most women wild. Yet there was something about the eyes that condemned artifice. An assessing, almost analytical directness that was disturbing.

Had he followed her? She cast his trolley a cursory glance and noted a collection of the usual food staples. Perhaps not.

Humour was a useful weapon. The edges of her mouth tilted slightly. 'Ice cream,' she acknowledged with a trace of flippancy. 'Vanilla, with caramel and double chocolate chip.'

Dark eyes gleamed, and his deep husky laughter did strange things to her equilibrium.

'Ah, the lady has a sweet tooth.'

There was a ring on her left hand, and he wondered at his stab of disappointment. His cutting edge style of wheeling and dealing in the business arena hadn't stemmed from hesitation. He didn't hesitate now.

He reached forward and placed a light finger against the wide filigree gold band. 'Does this have any significance?'

Francesca snatched her hand from the trolley. 'Whether it does or not is none of your business.'

So she had a temper to go with that glorious dark auburn hair, Dominic mused, and wondered if her passion matched it. His interest intensified. 'Indulge me.'

She wanted to turn and walk away, but something made her stay. 'Give me one reason why I should?'

'Because I don't poach another man's possession.' The words held a lethal softness that bore no hint of apology, and his expression held a dispassionate watchfulness as she struggled to restrain her anger.

Dignity was the key, and she drew in a calming breath, then slowly raked her eyes over his tall frame from head to foot, and back again.

'Attractive packaging,' she accorded with silky detachment. She met his gaze squarely and held it. 'However, I have no interest in the contents.'

'Pity,' he drawled. 'The discovery could prove fascinating.' There was droll humour apparent, and something else she couldn't define. 'For both of us.'

'In your dreams,' she dismissed sweetly. The check-out lane was located at the far end of the aisle, and she had everything she needed.

He made no effort to stop her as she moved away, yet for one infinitesimal moment she'd had the feeling he'd seen into the depths of her soul, acknowledged her secrets, staked a claim and retreated, sure of his ability to conquer.

Insane, Francesca mentally chastised herself as she loaded carrybags into the boot and returned the trolley. Then she slid in behind the wheel of her car and switched on the ignition.

She was tired, wired. The first was the direct result of a long flight; she owed the second to a man she never wanted to meet again.

Re-entering the apartment, she stowed her purchases into the refrigerator and pantry. Rejecting coffee or tea, she filled a glass with iced water and drank half the contents before crossing to the telephone.

Fifteen minutes later she'd connected with each parent and made arrangements to see them. Next, she punched in the digits necessary to connect with Laraine, her agent.

Business. For the past three years it had been her salvation. Travelling the world, an elegant clotheshorse for the top fashion designers. She had the face, the figure, and the essential *élan.* But for how long would she remain one of the coveted few? More importantly, did she *want* to?

There were young waifs clamouring in the wings, eager for fame and fortune. Designers always had an eye for the look, and the excitement of a fresh new face.

Fashion was fickle. *Haute couture* a viperish nest of designer ego fed by prestigious clientele, the press, and the copy merchants.

Yet amongst the outrageousness, the hype and the glitter, there was pleasure in displaying the visual artistry of imaginative design. Satisfaction when it all came together to form something breathtakingly spectacular.

It made the long flights, living out of a suitcase in one hotel room or another, cramped backstage changing rooms, the *panic* that invariably abounded behind the scenes worthwhile. A cynic wouldn't fail to add that an astronomical modelling fee helped lessen the pain.

Financial security was something Francesca had enjoyed for as long as she could remember. As a child, there had been a beautiful home, live-in help, and expensive private schooling. Yet, while her mother had perpetuated the fairytale existence, her father had ensured his daughter's feet remained firmly on the ground.

There were investments, property, and an enviable blue chip share portfolio, the income from which precluded a need to supplement it in any way.

Yet the thought of becoming a social butterfly with no clear purpose to the day had never appealed.

Perhaps it was her father's inherited Italian genes that kept the adrenalin flowing and provided the incentive to put every effort into a chosen project. 'Failure' didn't form part of her father's vocabulary.

Which brought Francesca back to the present. 'A week's grace,' she insisted, and listened to her agent's smooth plea to reconsider. 'Tomorrow morning we'll confer over coffee. Your office. Shall we say ten?'

She replaced the receiver, stretched her arms high, and felt the weariness descend. She'd make something light for dinner, then she'd undress and slip beneath the sheets of her comfortable bed.

CHAPTER TWO

FRANCESCA leaned across the desk in her agent's elegantly appointed office and traced a list of proposed modelling assignments with a milk-opal-lacquered nail.

'Confirm the cancer charity luncheon, the Leukaemia Foundation dinner. I'll do Tony's photo shoot, and I'll judge the junior modelling award, attend the gala lunch on the Gold Coast.' She paused, considered three invitations and dismissed two. 'The invitation-only showing at Margo's Double Bay boutique.' She picked up her glass of iced water and took an appreciative sip. 'That's it.'

'Anique Sorensen is being persuasive and persistent,' Laraine relayed matter-of-factly.

The fact that Francesca was known to donate half her appearance fee whenever she flew home between seasons invariably resulted in numerous invitations requesting her presence at various functions, all in aid of one charity or another.

'When?'

'Monday, Marriott Hotel.'

'Tell me it's for a worthwhile cause, and I'll kill you.'

'Then I'm dead. It's for the Make-A-Wish Foundation® of Australia.'

'Damn,' Francesca accorded inelegantly, wrinkling her nose in silent admonition of Laraine's widening smile.

'But you'll do it,' the agent said with outward satisfaction.

'Yes.' Francesca stood to her feet, collected her bag and slid the strap over one shoulder. She had a particular sympathy for terminally ill children. 'Fax me the details.'

'What are your plans for the rest of the day?'

'A secluded beach,' she enlightened. 'A good book, and the mobile phone.'

'Don't forget the block-out sunscreen.'

Francesca's smile held a teasing quality. 'Got it.'

An hour later she sat munching an apple beneath a sun umbrella on a northern beach gazing over the shoreline to the distant horizon.

There was a faint breeze wafting in from the ocean, cooling the sun's heat. She could smell the salt-spray, and there was the occasional cry from a lonely seagull as it explored the damp sand at the edge of an outgoing tide.

The solitude soothed and relaxed her, smoothing the edges of mind and soul.

Reflections were often painful, and with a determined effort Francesca extracted her book and read for an hour, then she retrieved a banana and a peach from her bag and washed both down with a generous amount of bottled water.

Phone calls. The first of which was to a dear friend with whom she'd shared boarding school during emotionally turbulent years when each had battled a stepmother and the effects of a dysfunctional family relationship.

She punched in the number, got past Reception, then a secretary, and chuckled at Gabbi's enthusiastic greeting and a demand as to when they would get together.

'Tonight, if you and Benedict are attending Leon's exhibition.'

The flamboyant gallery owner was known for his *soirées*, invitations to which featured high on the social calendar among the city's fashionable élite.

'You are? That's great,' Francesca responded with enthusiasm. 'I'm meeting Mother for dinner first, so I could be late.'

'Have fun,' Gabbi issued lightly, and Francesca laughed outright at the unspoken nuance in those two words.

It *was* fun listening to Sophy's breathy gossip over chicken consommé, salad and fruit. Sophy's permanent diet involved minuscule portions of fat-free calorie-depleted food.

A gifted raconteur, she had a wicked way with words that was endearingly humorous, and it was little wonder her mother gathered men as some women collected jewellery. All of whom remained friends long after the relationship had ended. With the exception of Rick, her first husband and Francesca's father. He was the one who had remained impervious to Sophy's machinations.

It was after nine when the waiter brought the bill, which Francesca paid, and she saw Sophy into a cab before crossing to her car.

Twenty minutes later she searched for an elusive parking space within walking distance of Leon's fashionable Double Bay gallery, located one, and made her way towards the brightly lit main entrance.

There were people everywhere, milling, drinking, and it was difficult to distinguish the muted baroque music beneath audible snatches of conversation.

'Francesca, *darling*!'

Leon—who else? She acknowledged his effusive greeting and allowed him to clasp her shoulders as he regarded her features with thoughtful contemplation.

'You must have a drink before you circulate.'

Her eyes assumed a humorous gleam. 'That bad, huh?'

'*Non*. But a glass in the hand—' He paused to effect a Gallic shrug. 'You can pretend, *oui*, that it is something other than mineral water.' He lifted a hand in imperious summons, and a waiter appeared out of nowhere, tray in hand.

Dutifully, she extracted a tall glass. 'Anything in particular you can recommend to add to my collection?'

'A sculpture,' Leon announced at once. 'It is a little raw, you understand, but the talent—' He touched fingers to his lips and blew a kiss into the air. '*Très magnifique*. In a few years it will be worth ten, twenty times what is being asked for it now.' He smiled, and brushed gentle knuckles to her cheek. 'Go, *cherie*, and examine. Exhibit Fourteen. It may not capture you immediately, but it grows, fascinates.'

An accurate description, Francesca accorded several minutes later, unsure of the sculpture's appeal.

Yet there was something that drew her attention again and again.

Leon was an expert in the art world, she trusted his judgement, and owned, thanks to his advice, several items which had increased dramatically in value since their date of purchase. Therefore, she would browse among the other exhibits, then return and perhaps view it from a fresh angle. It was certainly different from anything she owned.

There were a few fellow guests whose features were familiar, and she smiled, greeted several by name, paused to exchange polite conversation, then moved on, only to divert from her intended path as she glimpsed the endearingly familiar features of an attractive blonde threading a path towards her.

'Francesca!'

'Gabbi.'

They embraced, and tumbled into speech. 'It's so good to see you.'

'And you. Where's Benedict?' It was unlike Gabbi's husband to be far from his wife's side.

'Eyes right, about ten feet distant.'

Francesca caught the dry tone and conducted a casual sweeping glance in the indicated direction. Benedict's tall, dark-haired frame came into view, together with that of a familiar female form. Annaliese Schubert, a model with whom she'd shared a few catwalks both home and abroad.

'Your dear stepsister is in town, and bent on creating her usual mayhem?' An attempt to seduce Benedict Nicols appeared Annaliese's prime motivation. That she had been unsuccessful both before and after Benedict's marriage didn't appear to bother her in the slightest.

'Perceptive of you,' Gabbi replied wryly. 'How was Rome?'

Francesca hesitated fractionally, unaware of the fleeting darkness that momentarily clouded her eyes. 'The catwalks were exhausting.' Her shoulders lifted slightly, then fell. 'And Mario's mother lost a long battle with cancer.'

Empathetic understanding didn't require words, and Francesca was grateful Gabbi refrained from uttering more than the customary few.

'Let's do lunch,' Gabbi suggested gently. 'Is tomorrow too soon?'

'Done.'

'Good,' Gabbi said with satisfaction. She tucked a hand through Francesca's arm. 'Shall we examine the art exhibits for any hidden talent?'

They wandered companionably, slowly circling the room, and when Gabbi paused to speak to a friend Francesca moved forward to give closer scrutiny to a canvas that displayed a visual cacophony of bold colour.

She tilted her head in an attempt to fathom some form or symmetry that might make sense.

'It's an abstract,' a slightly accented male voice revealed with a degree of musing mockery.

Francesca's stomach muscles tightened, premonition providing an advance warning even as she turned slowly towards him.

The bank, the foodhall, and now the art gallery?

Dominic had witnessed her entrance, and noted her progress around the room with interest. And a degree of satisfaction when she was greeted with such enthusiasm by the wife of one of his business associates. It made it so much easier to initiate an introduction.

She regarded him silently. The deeply etched male features, the hard-muscled frame tamed somewhat beneath superb tailoring. Also apparent were the hand-stitched shoes, Hermes tie, and gold Rolex.

The smile reached his eyes, tingeing them with humour, yet there was a predatory alertness beneath the surface that was at variance with his portrayed persona.

A man who knew who he was, and didn't require any status symbols to emphasise his wealth or masculinity.

Power emanated from every pore, leashed and under control. Yet there was a hint of the primitive, a dramatic mesh of animalistic magnetism that stirred something within her, tripping the pulse and increasing her heartbeat.

'Francesca.'

The soft American drawl caught her attention, and she turned at once, her expression alive with delight.

'Benedict!' Her smile held genuine warmth as she leaned forward to accept his salutary kiss. 'It's been a while.'

'Indeed.' Gabbi's husband offered an affectionate smile in acknowledgement before shifting his attention to the man at her side. 'You've met Dominic?'

'It appears I'm about to.'

Something flickered in Benedict's eyes, then it was masked. 'Dominic Andrea. Francesca Angeletti.'

The mention of her surname provided the key to her identity, Dominic acknowledged, as details fell into place.

He was Greek, Francesca mused, not Italian. And the two men were sufficiently comfortable with each other to indicate an easy friendship.

'Francesca.'

Her name on his lips sounded—*different*. Sexy, evocative, alluring. And she didn't want to be any one of those things with any man. Especially not *this* man.

Dominic wondered if she was aware the fine gold flecks in her eyes intensified when she was defensive...and trying hard to hide it? He felt something stir deep inside, aside from the desire to touch his mouth to her own, to explore and possess it.

'Are you sufficiently brave to offer an opinion on my exhibit?'

He couldn't be serious? 'I'd prefer to opt out on the grounds that anything I say might damage your ego.'

His husky laughter sent a shivery sensation down the length of her spine. 'Benedict and Gabbi must bring you to dinner tomorrow night.'

If Dominic Andrea thought she'd calmly tag along he was mistaken! 'Why?'

'You intrigue me.' He saw her pupils dilate, sensed the uncertainty beneath her cool façade. And was curious to discover the reason.

'No. Thank you,' she added.

'Not curious to see my artist's attic?'

'Where you live doesn't interest me.' Nor do you, she wanted to add. And knew she lied. For there was an invisible pull of the senses, a powerful dynamism impossible to ignore.

A man who sought to forge his own destiny, she perceived, not at all fooled by the smile curving that generous mouth. The eyes were too dark and discerning, *dangerous*.

She had the strangest feeling she should be afraid of the knowledge evident in those depths. An instinctive sureness that he was intent on being a major force in her life.

'Six-thirty. Gabbi will give you the address.' His lips tilted slightly as he slanted her a mocking glance. 'If you'll excuse me?'

'Extraordinary man,' Francesca commented, silently adding lethal and persistent as she watched him thread his way to the opposite side of the gallery.

'A very successful one,' Benedict informed her mildly. 'Who dabbles in art and donates a lot of his work to charity.'

'Accept Dominic's invitation,' Gabbi added persuasively. 'If you don't, I'll be outnumbered, and the conversation will be confined to business.'

Francesca rolled her eyes. 'Not really a hardship. You excel in business.'

Gabbi's eyes sparkled with impish humour. 'Take a walk on the wild side and say *yes*. You might enjoy yourself.'

All Francesca's instincts shrieked a silent denial. She liked her life as it was, and didn't need nor want any complications that might upset its even tenure.

Although it might prove a challenge to play Dominic Andrea at his own game and win.

'What do you think of that sculpture in steel?' Benedict queried, successfully diverting their attention.

Ten minutes later Francesca chose to leave, indicating to Gabbi quietly, 'I'll see you at lunch tomorrow.'

Leon was effusive as she crossed to his side and thanked him for the invitation, and as she turned towards the door she saw Dominic Andrea deep in conversation with a stunning diminutive blonde.

Almost as if he sensed her gaze, his head lifted and dark eyes pierced hers with mesmerising awareness.

There was nothing overt in his expression, just an unwavering knowledge that had an electric effect on her equilibrium. It was almost as if he was staking a claim. Issuing a silent message that he would enjoy the fight, and the victory.

Fanciful imagination, Francesca dismissed as she gained the foyer, then she descended the short flight of steps and took the well-lit path to her car.

With the ignition engaged, she eased the vehicle forward and entered the busy thoroughfare.

Dominic Andrea had no part in her life, she assured herself silently as she headed towards her Double Bay apartment.

Francesca put the finishing touches to her make-up, examined the careless knot of hair she'd swept on top of her head, then stood back, pleased with the overall image.

Halter-necked black dress, sheer black tights, perilously high stiletto-heeled black pumps. Cosmetic artistry provided a natural look, and a brilliant red gloss coloured her lips. Jewellery comprised a diamond bracelet and matching ear-studs.

Without pausing to think, she collected a slim evening purse and car keys, walked out of the apartment and took the lift down to the basement car park.

Traffic was heavy as she drove through the city, and once clear of the Harbour Bridge she by-passed the expressway and headed towards Beauty Point.

Exclusive suburbs graced the city's northern shores, offering magnificent views over the inner harbour.

Dammit. *What was she doing?* Dressed to kill, on her way to attend a dinner she had no inclination to share with a man she hadn't wanted to see again.

She could turn back and go home, ring and apologise, using any one of several plausible excuses.

So why didn't she? Instead of turning between wrought-iron gates guarding an imposing concrete-textured Caribbean-style home situated at the crest of a semi-circular driveway?

All because of Gabbi's subtle challenge issued the previous evening, and endorsed and encouraged over lunch. Now it was a little late to have second thoughts.

Francesca parked behind Benedict's sporty

Jaguar and cast a quick glance at the digital clock before she switched off the engine.

Perfect. By the time she emerged from the car and walked the few steps to the front door, she would be ten minutes late.

A silent statement that she was here on her own terms.

Subdued melodic chimes echoed as she depressed the doorbell, and seconds later the thick, panelled door swung open to reveal a middle-aged housekeeper.

'Miss Angeletti? Please come in.'

High ceilings and floor-to-ceiling glass created a sense of spaciousness and light, with folding white-painted wooden shutters. Expensive art adorned the walls, and there were several Oriental rugs adorning pale cream marble floors.

She was escorted into a large lounge where Dominic's tall frame drew her attention like a magnet.

Dark trousers and a casual blue shirt lent an elegance she knew to be deceiving, for beneath the sophisticated veneer there was strength, not only of body but of mind.

'Please accept my apologies.'

Dominic's dark eyes held hers, quiet, still. He wasn't fooled in the slightest, but his voice was smooth as silk as he moved forward to greet her. 'Accepted.' He swept an arm towards a soft-cushioned leather sofa. 'Come and sit down.'

She crossed to a single chair and sank into it with elegant economy of movement.

A further insistence on independence? 'What can I offer you to drink?'

Something with a kick in it would be nice. Instead, she offered him a singularly sweet smile. 'Chilled water, with ice.'

'Sparkling or still?'

She resisted the temptation to request a specific brand-name. 'Still. Thank you.'

There was that glance again, laser-sharp beneath dark lashes, the slight lift of one eyebrow before he crossed to the cabinet.

Benedict looked mildly amused, and Gabbi shook her head in silent remonstrance. Francesca merely smiled.

Dominic returned and placed a tall glass within her reach on the side table.

'Thank you.' So achingly polite. *Too* polite?

Within minutes the housekeeper appeared to announce the meal was served, and they made their way into a large dining room adjacent to the lounge.

The table was beautifully set with white damask, on which reposed fine china, silver cutlery and stemmed crystal glasswear.

Francesca's gaze idly skimmed the mahogany chiffonnier, the long buffet cabinet, the elegantly designed chairs, and silently applauded his taste in furniture. And in soft furnishings, for the drapes and carpet were uniform in colour, the contrast supplied by artwork and mirrors adorning the walls.

Dominic seated Francesca beside him, opposite Gabbi and Benedict.

The courses were varied, and many, and, while exquisitely presented, they were the antithesis of designer food. There was, however, an artistically displayed platter of salads decorated with avocado, mango, and a sprinkling of pine nuts.

A subtle concession to what Dominic suspected was a model's necessity to diet?

Francesca always ate wisely and well, with little need to watch her intake of food. Tonight, however, she forked dainty portions from each course.

'You have a beautiful home.' The compliment was deserved, and she cast a glance towards the original artwork gracing the walls. Not any of them bore the distinctive style of the abstract she'd sighted at Leon's gallery.

As if reading her mind, Dominic enlightened musingly, 'I keep my work in the studio.'

One eyebrow lifted, and her voice held a hint of mockery. 'Is that a subtle invitation to admire your etchings?'

His fingers brushed her wrist as he leaned forward to replenish her glass with water, and a chill shiver feathered its way over the surface of her skin in silent recognition of something deeply primitive.

The knowledge disturbed her, and her eyes were faintly wary as they met his.

'The expected cliché?' The drawled query held wry humour, and his eyes held a warmth she didn't care to define. 'At the risk of disappointing you, I paint in the studio and confine lovemaking to the bedroom.'

Something curled inside her stomach, and she lifted her glass and took a generous swallow before setting it down onto the table. 'How—prosaic.'

His husky chuckle held quizzical amusement,

and an indolent smile broadened the sensual curve of his mouth. 'Indeed? You don't think comfort is a prime consideration?'

The image of a large bed, satin sheets, and leisurely languorous foreplay sprang to mind...a damning and totally unwarranted vision she wanted no part of.

Francesca had a desire to give a stinging response, and probably would have if they'd been alone. Instead, she aimed for innocuous neutrality, and tempered it with a totally false smile that didn't fool anyone, least of all Dominic, in the slightest. 'Not always.'

'The chicken is delicious.' Dear sweet Gabbi, who sought to defuse the verbal direction of their exchange.

Francesca cast her a sweeping glance that issued a silent statement—*I'm having fun*. And saw her friend's eyes widen fractionally in answering warning.

'How was your trip to Italy, Francesca?' Benedict issued the bland query. 'Were you able to spend any time outside Rome?'

She decided to play the social conversational game. 'No,' she enlightened evenly. 'However, I'm due in Milan next month for the European spring collections.' Closely followed by Paris.

Her life was like riding a merry-go-round...big cities, bright lights, the adrenalin rush. Then, every so often, she stepped off and took time out in normality. A vacation abroad, or, more often than not, she flew home to spend time with family and friends. They were her rock, the one thing constant in her life she could rely on.

'You enjoy the international scene?'

Francesca turned slightly to the man seated at her side, glimpsed the remarkable steadiness in his gaze—and something else she was unable to interpret. 'Yes.'

'Would you care for more salad?'

A subtle reminder that she was scarcely doing the sumptuous selection of food much justice? It hardly made sense that she was deliberately projecting the image of a diet fanatic, but there was a tiny gremlin urging her to travel a mildly outrageous path.

'Thank you.' She reached for the utensils and placed a modest serving onto her plate, then proceeded to fork small portions with delicate precision.

There was a dessert to die for reposing on the chiffonnier, and she spared the exquisitely decorated torte a regretful glance. A slice of mouthwatering ambrosia she'd have to forego the pleasure of savouring in order to continue the expected accepted image.

'Did Leon manage to sell your abstract?' She sounded facetious, and felt a momentary pang for the discourtesy.

'It wasn't for sale,' Dominic relayed with seemingly careless disregard, and smiled as her eyebrows arched in silent query.

'Really?' Francesca let her gaze encompass his rugged features and lingered on the strong bone structure before meeting the musing gleam in those dark eyes. 'You don't *look* like an artist.'

His mouth quirked slightly at the edges. 'How, precisely, is your impression of an artist supposed to look?'

Harmless words, but she was suddenly conscious of an elevated nervous tension that had no known basis except a strong, instinctive feeling that she was playing a dangerous game with a man well-versed in every aspect of the hunt.

Akin to a predator prepared to watch and wait as his prey gambolled foolishly within sight, aware that the time was of his choosing, the kill a foregone conclusion.

Now you're being fanciful, she chided, suddenly angry with herself for lapsing into an idiotic mind game.

'Shall we move to the lounge for coffee?' Dominic suggested with deceptive mildness.

In a way it was a relief to shift location, and she breathed a silent sigh as the evening moved towards a close.

The impish gremlin was still in residence as she declined coffee and requested tea. 'Herbal, if you have it.' Long lashes gave an imperceptible flutter, then swept down to form a protective veil.

'Of course.' The request didn't faze him in the least. It was almost as if he'd been prepared for it, and within minutes she nursed a delicate cup filled with clear brown liquid she had no inclination to taste.

Terrible, she conceded as she studiously sipped the innocent brew. And smiled as Gabbi, Benedict and Dominic savoured dark, aromatic coffee she would have much preferred to drink.

Hoist by her own petard, Francesca acknowledged with rueful acceptance. It served her right.

'Another cup?'

Not if she could help it! 'Thank you, no. That was delicious.'

Benedict rose to his feet in one smooth movement, his eyes enigmatic as they met those of his wife. 'If you'll excuse us, Dominic?'

'It's been a lovely evening,' Gabbi said gently as she collected her purse.

Their imminent departure provided an excellent excuse for Francesca to leave. It was what Dominic expected. But she was damned if she'd give him the satisfaction.

Fool, she mentally chastised herself as he escorted Gabbi and Benedict to the front door. Pick up your evening bag and follow them.

Too late, she decided a few minutes later when he returned to the lounge.

Francesca watched as he folded his lengthy frame into a cushioned chair directly opposite.

'Your friendship with Gabbi is a long-standing one?'

'Are you going to express a need to explore my background?'

'Not particularly.'

'No request for an in-depth profile?' she queried drily.

Dominic was silent for several seemingly long seconds, wanting to tear down the barrier she'd erected but aware of the need for caution and a degree of patience. 'I'm aware of the professional one,' he drawled with assumed indolence. 'Tell me about your marriage.'

She stopped breathing, felt the pressure build, and sought to expel it slowly. She wanted to serve him a volley of angry words, throw something, *anything* that would release some of her pain. Instead, she resorted to stinging mockery.

'Gabbi failed to fill you in?'

His eyes were steady. 'Minimum details.'

'It can be encapsulated in one sentence: *champion racing car driver Mario Angeletti killed on the Monaco Grand Prix circuit within months of his marriage to international model Francesca Cardelli.*'

Three years had passed since that fateful day. Yet the vivid horror remained. It didn't matter that she hadn't personally witnessed the tearing of metal, the disintegration of car and man as fuel ignited in catastrophic explosion. Television news cameras, newspaper photographs and graphic journalistic reports ensured no detail remained unrecorded.

Family and close friends had shielded her, protecting and nurturing during the emotional fall-out. And afterwards she had stepped back onto the catwalk, aware every move, every nuance of her expression was being carefully watched for visible signs of distress.

Some had even attempted to provoke it. Yet not once had she let down her guard. Only those who knew her well saw the smile didn't quite reach her eyes, and recognised the smooth social patter as a practised façade.

'It must have been a very painful time for you.'

Francesca was unable to verbally denounce his sympathy, for there was none. Merely an empathetic statement that ignored conventional platitudes.

'Would you like a drink? Some more tea, coffee?' The smile held musing warmth. 'Something stronger, perhaps?'

Francesca stood to her feet, her expression wary as he mirrored her action. 'I really must leave.'

'Do I frighten you?' The query was voiced in a soft drawl, and succeeded in halting her steps.

No doubt about it, his target aim was deadly.

'Fear' was a multi-faceted word that encompassed many emotions. Slowly she turned towards him and met his gaze. Her chin tilted fractionally. A mental stiffening of her own resources? 'No.'

His eyes never left hers, but she felt as if he'd stripped every protective layer she'd swathed around her frozen heart and laid it bare and bleeding.

Oh, God, what was happening here? She'd known he was trouble the first time she saw him. *Walk away,* a tiny voice bade silently. *Now.*

A faint smile curved the edges of that sensual mouth, and there was a transitory gleam of humour apparent in the depth of those dark eyes. 'I'm relieved to hear it.'

'Why?' The demand seemed perfectly logical.

He looked at her carefully, weighing his words and assessing the damage they might do. And how he would deal with it. 'I want you,' he stated gently, lifting a hand to trace a gentle forefinger down the edge of her cheek.

His touch was like fire, and her pulse jumped, then raced to a quickened beat, almost as if in silent recognition of something she refused to acknowledge.

'Tangled sheets and an exchange of body fluids?' Inside, her emotions were shredding into pieces. Her eyes seared his, and her chin tilted fractionally as she took a step away from him. 'I don't *do* one-night stands.'

Courage. And passion. Banked, reserved. But there. He wanted it all. And knew she'd fight him every inch of the way.

'Neither do I.'

His words sent a shiver feathering down the length of her spine. What was it with this man? She found it annoying that just as she was about to categorise him, he shifted stance.

Dominic watched the play of emotions in her expressive eyes. No matter how much he wanted it to be different, he could wait. The temptation to pull her up against him and let her feel the effect she had on him was strong. To cover her mouth with his own, explore and vanquish.

He did neither. It would keep. Until the next time. And he'd ensure there was a next time.

Francesca felt the need to escape, and good manners instilled since childhood ensured she uttered a few polite words in thanks.

'Why, when you merely sampled a bird-like portion from each course, then picked at the salad?'

She experienced a momentary tinge of remorse

for the manner in which she'd eaten the delectable food. Did he suspect it had been deliberate? Somehow she had the instinctive feeling he saw too much, *knew* too much of the human psyche.

'My loss of appetite bore no reflection on your housekeeper's culinary ability.'

'In that case, I'll refer the compliment.'

Francesca turned and walked from the room to the front door, acutely aware of his presence at her side. She paused as he reached forward to pull back one of the large, panelled doors.

'What were you doing shopping for food in a supermarket when you employ a housekeeper?'

He could have used any one of several glib excuses, or employed a deliberately flattering remark. Instead he chose honesty. 'I wanted to see you again.'

Her stomach lurched, and an icy chill feathered her skin at the directness of his gaze.

'Goodnight.' She moved past him and stepped quickly down to her car, unlocked it and slid in behind the wheel.

The engine fired with a refined purr, and she resisted the temptation to speed down the driveway, choosing instead to ease the vehicle through the gates onto the road before quickly accelerating towards the main arterial road leading towards the Harbour Bridge.

Damn him. Francesca's fingers tightened on the steering wheel until her knuckles shone white. He was fast proving to be an intrusive force—one she didn't need in her life.

The sky was a deep indigo-blue sprinkled with

stars, and beneath them lay the city, dark velvet laced by a tracery of electric lights that had no discernible pattern. Bright neon flashed, providing vivid colour as one advertisement vied with another. A commuter train slipped by in electronic silence, its carriages illuminated and partly empty.

It was still early, yet there was already action in the city streets. Professionals worked the pavements, hustling and touting and evading the law as they mingled with the tourists and the curious.

Francesca took the expressway through the Domain, bypassed Kings Cross and headed towards the main arterial road leading to Double Bay.

Her head felt heavy, and she would have given much to be able to stop the car and walk in the clear night air. Instead she drove to her apartment building, garaged the car, then rode the lift to her designated floor.

A leisurely cool shower followed by an iced drink while she viewed television would have to suffice.

Yet nothing provided a distraction from the man who disturbed her thoughts.

Sleep didn't come easily, and even when it did, there were jagged dreams that made little sense. Except one, from which she awoke damp-skinned and damp-eyed. A vivid recall of Mario's laughing features as he stepped into his racing-car and donned his helmet prior to lining up for the last race of his life.

On the other side of the city Dominic stood looking out at the glittering lights across a darkened harbour as he reflected on the woman who had not long driven away from his home.

Sleep was elusive. At worst he could make do with six hours, five if he had to. Tonight he had the feeling he'd have to manage with less.

The fax machine shrilled in another room, and he ignored it.

What he needed was a carefully constructed strategy. A campaign that would leave nothing to chance.

Tomorrow he would make a call to Benedict Nicols in the hope that Gabbi might be persuaded to reveal details of Francesca's social calendar.

Subterfuge was permissible in the pursuit of an objective.

CHAPTER THREE

THE next few days were relaxing as Francesca caught up with friends, did some shopping, and enjoyed a rescheduled lunch with her father in an exclusive restaurant close to his office building.

The food was excellent, the ambience superb.

'How is Madeline?' Her stepmother was hardly the wicked kind, but Madeline viewed Francesca as a contestant for Rick's affections, and waged a subtle war to test her husband's priorities whenever Francesca was in town.

'Fine.' The warmth in his voice was unmistakable, and as long as Francesca continued to hear it she was prepared to forgive Madeline almost anything.

'And Katherine and John?' They were close, and Francesca regarded them as sister and brother rather than step-siblings. 'We must get together.'

'Is tonight too soon?' her father queried with a degree of wry humour. 'Katherine has, she assures me, an outfit to die for, and John seems convinced a new suit will elevate him in years to the enviable position of escorting his famed stepsister to an élite restaurant, where, God willing, some super-vigilant photographer will take a photo which will appear in tomorrow's newspaper, whereupon he'll be the most sought-after beau of the student ball.'

Francesca laughed. A glorious, warm, husky

sound. 'I take it I should wear something incredibly glamorous?'

Rick Cardelli's smile held philosophical humour. 'Obscenely so, I imagine,' he said drily.

Concern clouded her features. 'I don't want to overshadow Katherine.' Or Madeline.

His dark eyes gleamed, and the edges of his mouth curved upward. 'My dear Francesca, Katherine wants you to shine—vividly.'

'Done.' Francesca lifted her glass and touched it to the rim of her father's wine glass. '*Salute*, Papà,' she said solemnly.

'*Ecco*. Health and happiness,' he added gently.

She picked up her cutlery and speared a succulent prawn from its bed of cos lettuce decorated with slices of avocado and mango. The dressing was divine, and she savoured every mouthful.

They were halfway through the main course when Francesca became aware of a strange prickling sensation at the back of her neck.

Almost as if she was being watched.

Recognition was an aspect of her profession that she had come to terms with several years ago, and she dealt with it with practised charm.

But this was different. Mild interest in her presence didn't usually elicit this heightened sense of awareness, an acute alertness, as if something deep inside was forcing her attention.

She turned slowly, allowing her gaze to idly skim the room. And came to a sudden halt as she caught sight of Dominic Andrea sharing a table with two men a few metres from her own.

At that moment he glanced up, and her eyes collided with his dark, piercing gaze. He offered a slow, musing smile, which merely earned him a brief nod before she returned her attention to the contents on her plate.

Her appetite diminished so as to be almost non-existent, and she declined dessert, choosing to settle for coffee.

'Francesca?'

She looked up at the sound of her name and realised she hadn't taken in a word her father had said. 'I'm sorry, what did you say?'

'Is there a reason for your distraction?' Rick queried, and she wrinkled her nose in wry humour.

'An unwanted one.'

Her father chuckled. 'Now that I have your attention...Madeline would like you to join us at home for dinner. Does Wednesday suit?'

'I'll look forward to it.'

The waiter cleared their table and brought coffee.

Francesca was conscious of every movement she made, aware as she had never been before of one man's veiled scrutiny.

No one would have guessed to what degree Dominic's presence bothered her, or how much she longed to escape.

'A refill?'

'No, thanks.' She cast her father a warm smile. 'This has been lovely.' She watched as he summoned the waiter to bring the bill.

'Rick. How are you?'

Even if the faint aroma of exclusive male cologne hadn't warned her, the slow curl in the pit of her stomach did.

Dominic Andrea. Dark eyes, inscrutable expression behind the warm smile.

'Francesca.' The intimate inflexion he gave her name made the hairs at her nape rise in protest. Something that irritated the hell out of her and lent a very polite edge to her voice as she acknowledged his presence.

Dominic leaned down and brushed his lips against her temple. The contact was brief, his touch light. But something ignited and flared through her veins, potent, alive—*electric*.

She wanted to kill him. In fact, she definitely would kill him the next time she saw him. *If* she saw him again. How *dare* he imply an intimacy that didn't exist? Would never exist.

'You know each other?' Rick queried, interested in the expressive play of emotions that chased fleetingly across his daughter's features.

'We dined together earlier in the week,' Dominic enlightened smoothly.

Damning. Francesca cursed, all too aware of his intended implication.

'Really?' Rick absorbed the information and wondered whether anything was to be made of it. 'You'll join us for coffee?'

'I'm with two colleagues. Another time, perhaps?' His eyes shifted to Francesca, who met his steady gaze with equanimity. 'If you'll excuse me?'

He reminded her of a sleeping tiger. All leashed power beneath the guise of relaxed ease.

Francesca watched as he turned and threaded his way back to his table.

'I didn't realise you were on such close terms with Dominic Andrea. I have one of his paintings.'

She couldn't imagine her father coveting anything resembling the colourful abstract resting in Leon's gallery. A mental run-through of the artwork gracing Rick and Madeline's walls brought a mental blank.

'The vase of roses in the dining room,' Rick enlightened. 'Madeline assures me it is perfect for the room.'

Francesca had to agree. She'd silently admired it numerous times. Such painstaking brushwork, a delicate blending of colours. Velvet curling petals, the perfection of leaf foliage, the drops of fresh dew. Displayed in a glazed ceramic bowl against a shadowy background. The work of a man, she conceded, who possessed infinite patience and skill. Did those same qualities extend to pleasuring a woman? Somehow she imagined that they did.

Sensation feathered the surface of her skin, and she consciously banked down the acute ache deep within. She experienced guilt, and mentally attempted to justify it.

'Shall we leave?' Rick suggested as he settled the bill. Together they threaded their way towards the exit and parted with an affectionate kiss as they reached the pavement.

Shopping, a visit to the hairdresser and the beautician took care of the afternoon, then she drove home and dressed for the evening ahead.

Obscenely glamorous. Well, the gown was certainly that! Indigo lace over raw silk, form-fitting. A lace bolero, high-heeled pumps and evening purse. Her favourite perfume added a finishing touch.

Familial affection was in evidence during dinner, and Francesca relaxed in the warmth of it. There were gifts to distribute that she'd collected in Rome, and the photographer appeared at their table right on cue.

If Madeline knew it was a set-up, she didn't let on. It was enough that she and her children would appear on the social pages, their names in print.

Sunday brought abnormally high summer temperatures, and Francesca was glad she'd made arrangements to join her mother for a day cruising the harbour on a friend's boat. The breeze made for pleasant conditions, and for the first time in ages she slept the night through, rising later than usual the next morning at the start of what promised to be a hectic week.

Francesca drummed her fingers against the steering wheel in an increasingly agitated tattoo as it took two and sometimes three light changes to clear each computer-controlled intersection.

Traffic into the city was heavier than usual, and a silent curse formed on her lips as green changed to amber, then red.

In less than five minutes she was due to check in backstage in readiness to appear on the catwalk for a charity fashion parade.

The first of many she'd agreed to do during her stay on Australian shores.

Damn. Another red light. Was everything conspiring against her?

Ten minutes later she swept into the main entrance of the hotel, handed her keys to the valet,
took the parking stub, then hurriedly made her way
into the foyer.

The Grand Ballroom was situated on the first
level, and she tossed up whether to take the stairs
or the lift.

The stairs won, and minutes later she threaded
her way through milling guests to the main doors.
Inside uniformed waiters were conducting a last-
minute check of the tables, and harried committee
members conferred, consulted and made small
changes to existing seating arrangements.

'Francesca. *Darling!*' Six feet tall, Anique
Sorensen, society doyenne and leading fundraiser,
embraced her stature by clothing it as expensively
and outrageously as possible. This year the focus
appeared to be jewellery. Masses of gold chains
round her neck and adorning each wrist. On anyone
else it would have looked garish, even tacky. But
Anique managed to make it appear a fashion statement. 'I'm so grateful you can be here today. You
look fabulous. Just fabulous.' She paused to draw
breath and clasped Francesca close in a bear-hug,
then did the air-kiss thing before releasing her hold.
'How *are* you?'

Francesca said what she knew Anique expected
to hear...in one syllable. 'Fine. And you?'

'Ask me after the show.' The smile was in place,
but there was an edge to it. 'I'm waiting on two
models.'

A fashion showing might *look* smooth and display professional co-ordination out front, but organised chaos ruled behind the scenes.

'Traffic's heavy,' Francesca offered, shifting her garment bag from one shoulder to the other. 'Who?'

'Annaliese and Cassandra.'

Cassandra was a doll, laid-back, easy to get along with and professional. Annaliese, on the other hand, was a sultry cat who played diva to the hilt both on and off the catwalk.

'They'll be here,' Francesca assured her, and caught Anique's wry smile.

'I know, darling. But *when*?' Her sharp gaze circled the room. 'The guests are due to be seated any minute, in ten the compère will announce the charity's chairwoman's introductory speech, and five after that we need to roll.'

'It'll all come together.'

'It always does,' Anique agreed. 'I'd kill for a cigarette and a double gin.' She gave a long-suffering sigh. 'I swear, next year I'm not going to be on *any* committee.'

'You will. They need you.' It was true. 'No one can pull in the people the way you do.'

The eyes softened, their expression sincere. 'You're a sweet girl, Francesca.'

The usual bedlam reigned backstage, with racks of clothes and accessories and fellow models in various stages of undress fixing their make-up. Designers' assistants, co-ordinators, were each running numerous preliminary checks in the countdown to showtime.

Always there were last-minute changes, alterations that had to be noted on everyone's list. Mostly, they got it right.

Francesca checked the clothes and accessories she was to wear, and their sequence, then she shed her outer clothes and got to work on her make-up.

'Fran, sweetie.' Cassandra, tall, willowy and a natural blonde squeezed in to grab some mirror space. 'I need someone to tell me I'm sane.'

'You're sane,' Francesca said obligingly. 'That bad, huh?'

Cassandra delved into her make-up bag and seconds later her fingers flew with lightning speed, a touch of blusher here, eyeshadow there, and an experienced twist with the mascara wand. 'My daughter has tonsillitis, I broke a nail on the car door latch, snagged a run in my tights, and got caught in traffic.' She outlined her mouth and applied brilliant red gloss. 'Annaliese has yet to put in an appearance out front, and Anique...' She paused, and rolled her eyes in a wonderfully expressive gesture.

'Is about to go into orbit?' Francesca completed drily.

'You got it in one.'

The compère's introduction could be heard in the background. 'Five minutes,' one of the co-ordinators warned, whirling as a figure dressed entirely in scarlet flew into the room. 'Annaliese. You're impossibly late.'

The leggy, dark-haired model gave a careless shrug, tried to look apologetic and failed. 'Blame the cab-driver.'

'We'll run you last in the first segment,' the co-ordinator improvised. 'Just *hurry*, will you?' She altered her list, and moved quickly to ensure the alteration was duplicated.

Francesca stepped into casual shorts, secured them, added a top, and slid her feet into heeled slingback white sandals. Then she picked up the wraparound skirt and hitched it over one shoulder.

The chairwoman's speech finished, the compère completed his spiel, and the music began.

'OK, girls,' the co-ordinator announced. 'This is it. Cassandra, you first. Then Francesca.'

Upbeat music, flashing lights, *showtime*.

It was a familiar scene, different catwalk, another city. Francesca waited for her cue, smile in place, then she emerged on stage. Each movement was perfectly co-ordinated as she walked to the centre, paused, and turned before taking the catwalk. Choreographed action that displayed the clothes to their best advantage.

Resortwear, swimwear, city and career wear, collections, formal evening wear, bridal.

Designers fussed, assistants frowned, and the co-ordinators soothed and cajoled and kept everything moving smoothly.

Francesca effected one quick change after another, exchanging shoes, accessories. The bridalwear segment was the designers' *coup de grâce*, and each gown was modelled solo to give specific impact. Slow music and a slow pace down the length of the catwalk and back.

Then all the models appeared on stage together, the guests gave a noisy ovation, the compère wound down and the designers slipped out to stand beside the model wearing their creation. Then it was all over.

Waiters began appearing, bearing trays laden with plates of food, and drink waiters hovered unobtrusively as they took and delivered orders.

Francesca emerged backstage and began discarding the heavy satin beaded gown. Her own clothes felt comfortable by comparison, and she crossed to the mirror to tone down her make-up.

On the agenda was something light to eat, then she'd drive back to the apartment, change and swim a few leisurely lengths of the pool.

'Will you be at Margo's tomorrow?'

She glanced up at the sound of Cassandra's voice. 'Yes. You too?'

'Uh-huh.'

'I don't do it for free,' Annaliese declared in bored tones as she joined them.

'Really?' Cassandra queried sweetly, unable to let the unintentional *double entendre* escape unmentioned. 'As a matter of interest, how much do you charge?'

Francesca saw Annaliese's eyes narrow, glimpsed the anger tighten that full mouth. 'Jealous, *sweetie*?'

'Why, *no*, honey. I don't relish the attached strings.'

'Pity you didn't consider *strings* when you opted to travel the hard road as a single mother.'

Oh, my, Francesca accorded wryly. Much more of this and there would be a cat-fight.

'Annaliese, why don't you hush your mouth before I do it for you?' Cassandra queried silkily.

'One hopes that's an idle threat, darling. If not, let me warn that I wouldn't hesitate to lay assault charges.'

'Bitch,' Cassandra muttered as soon as Annaliese vacated the changing room. 'She likes to rattle my chain.'

'It's her favoured pastime,' Francesca enlightened as she collected her garment bag and slung it over one shoulder. 'I'm out of here.' Her lips curved into a generous smile. 'See you tomorrow.'

As she emerged from backstage Anique snagged her arm and heaped ebullient praise for a job well done.

Ever polite, Francesca paused to exchange a greeting with various women, some of whom she knew and others she did not. Consequently it seemed an age before she was able to escape into the main lobby and summon the valet to collect her car.

'A message for you, ma'am.'

Who? she queried silently as she took the envelope from the valet's hand. 'Thanks.' She switched on her mobile phone and checked her voicemail, then she lifted the envelope flap and extracted a business card.

Dominic Andrea's business card, with a message *Call me* penned on the back above a series of digits. Francesca didn't know whether to be annoyed or amused, and slipped the card into her bag as she stepped through the automatic sliding doors to wait for her car.

Within seconds it swept into the curved fore-

court. The valet jumped out and held open the door
as she slid in behind the wheel.

It took longer than usual to reach her apartment,
and once inside she tossed down her bag, slipped
off her shoes, then padded barefoot into the kitchen
for a cool drink.

Ten minutes later she took the lift down to the
ground floor and made her way towards the indoor
pool.

The soft, clear water relaxed her, easing the kinks
from tired muscles as she stroked several laps, then
she turned onto her back and allowed her body to
drift with the movement of the water for a while
before reversing her position.

Employing a slow breaststroke, she made her
way to the side and levered herself up onto the tiled
edge. Water streamed off her body as she stood to
her feet, and she caught up her towel and dealt with
the excess moisture.

It was almost five when she re-entered the apartment, and with automatic movements she crossed
into the bedroom, entered the *en suite* bathroom and
turned on the shower.

Ten minutes later she pulled on a towelling robe
and began blowdrying her hair, then she moved into
the kitchen to prepare something light to eat.

An omelette, she decided. Eaten in the lounge
while watching television.

The phone rang twice during the evening. Her
mother suggesting lunch, and Gabbi issuing an invitation to the theatre.

CHAPTER FOUR

MARGO'S boutique was one of several in the exclusive Double Bay boulevard catering to the city's rich and famous.

An astute woman with a love of fashion, Margo had opened the boutique soon after her husband's death in a bid to channel her energies into something constructive. Adhering to instinct, she stocked expensive designer originals that were classically elegant. Her window display held one mannequin, whose apparel was changed every day. A selection of bags were offered to complement designer shoes.

Margo's quarterly invitation-only fashion showings were offered to a valued clientele, with the request that they each bring a guest. Champagne and orange juice flowed, catered refreshments were served with coffee and tea. Margo offered a ten per cent reduction in price on everything in the shop and donated a further ten per cent of the day's take to her favoured charity.

A fondness for using fledgling unknown models had boosted the careers of several, a few of whom had gone on to achieve international recognition.

Francesca had been one of them. Hence, if a visit home coincided with one of Margo's showings, Francesca donated her services *sans* fee, out of respect and affection for a woman who gave far more to charity than was generally known, and who insisted such philanthrophic gestures were never reported in the press.

Parking wasn't a problem, and Francesca crossed the square at a brisk pace, dodging small puddles accumulated from an early-morning rainfall. An elegantly clad vendeuse stood at the door, welcoming guests and checking their invitations. Outside there was hired uniformed security.

Collectively, the jewellery adorning fingers, wrists, necks and earlobes would amount to a small fortune.

Francesca counted two Rolls-Royces and a Bentley lining the kerb, and three chauffeurs engaged in transferring their employers from car to pavement.

The boutique's air-conditioned interior provided a welcome contrast to the high humidity that threatened, according to the day's forecast, to climb into the nineties.

'Francesca.' Margo's greeting held warmth and genuine enthusiasm. 'It's so good to see you. Cassandra arrived a minute ago, and the three novices are already quaking out back.'

A smile tugged the edges of her mouth. 'Quaking?'

Margo's eyes held a musing sparkle. 'Almost literally. And desperately in need of professional wisdom to help put them at ease.'

Francesca thought back nine years to the time she had stood consumed by nerves in one of Margo's changing rooms for the first time and doubted *any* words would make a difference.

'I'll do my best.'

'I'm counting on it.'

Francesca moved through the vestibule to the changing rooms, greeted Cassandra, the co-ordinator assigned to accessorise each outfit and detail their order of appearance, and smiled at the three girls whose expressions bore witness to a sense of awe and trepidation.

They were so *young*. Humour was the only way to go, and her eyes assumed a mischievous sparkle. 'You've forgotten everything Margo said, are convinced your limbs will freeze the instant you go out there, and, failing that, you'll trip and fall flat on your face.' Her mouth curved with impish wit. 'Right? None of which is going to happen. Trust me.'

Margo was an exemplary organiser, and with plenty of staff on hand the fashion showing began without a hitch. Champagne flowed, and the guests were receptive. Seating was arranged three deep in two opposing semi-circles.

Francesca was first out, and she paused, executed a slow turn, then completed a round of the inner circle.

It was as she turned back to the audience that she saw him. Dominic Andrea, attired in a formal business suit, blue shirt, navy tie. Looking, she noted wryly, very comfortable with his surroundings, and not at all daunted at being only one of three men present in a room filled with women.

What the hell was he doing here?

Francesca's smile encompassed everyone and her eyes focused on no one in particular. Head held high, shoulders squared, she went through a familiar routine.

Yet she was acutely aware of the darkly attractive man whose attention she sensed rather than saw, and she had to actively steel herself against the faint shivering sensation that spiralled the length of her spine.

'What gives?'

Francesca cast Cassandra a harried glance as she slid down the zip fastening and stepped out of a tailored skirt. 'Be specific.' She unbuttoned the blouse and discarded it, then reached for an elegant trouser suit.

'There's a man seated third row, centre,' Cassandra declared as she donned tailored trousers and slid the zip in place, 'who seems to be showing an intense interest in your every move.'

As the morning progressed Francesca became increasingly aware of Dominic's presence. And his attention.

Why did she feel so *exposed* beneath his encompassing scrutiny? She hadn't felt this... 'Nervous' wasn't strictly accurate. She'd walked down too many catwalks, appeared at too many fashion showings to allow nerves to undermine professionalism.

Aware. That about summed it up. Attuned to one person to such an infinite degree that you were able to *sense* every glance without seeing it. The tingle that feathered down her spine, the slight heaviness of her breasts as each nipple tightened, and the slow, soft curling sensation deep within.

All this as a result of a few chance encounters

with the man, a few shared hours in company of mutual friends over dinner, and the brush of his lips against her temple? It was crazy.

Even more absurd was the feeling that she'd entered a one-way street from which there was no return.

Wayward thoughts, she dismissed. Her life was pleasant, she had command of it, and memories of Mario filled her heart. What more did she need?

Shared passion. A warm body to hold onto in the long night hours.

Where had that come from?

Fleeting pain darkened her eyes as guilt, remorse, *anger* tore at something deep inside, and for one split second she wanted to run and hide.

Yet she did neither. Professionalism ensured she tilted her head a fraction higher, curved her lips to make her smile a little brighter, and she walked, turned, paused with the ease of long practice.

Intimate, classy, *successful*, Francesca dubbed the event as it came to a close. Everyone bought. Garments, shoes, bags. Each was folded reverently in tissue paper and deposited into one of Margo's stylish carrybags.

Francesca pulled on an elegant Armani trouser suit, slid her feet into high-heeled pumps, then caught up her capacious carry-all and slid the wide strap over one shoulder.

She entered the salon, saw the number of guests milling in groups, and took a steadying breath as she glimpsed Dominic deep in conversation with an attractive woman on the other side of the room.

Why was he still here?

Almost as if he sensed her glance, he raised his head and cast her a penetrating look, then returned his attention to the woman beside him.

Shattering, Francesca perceived. The effect he had on her senses. She'd been supremely conscious of his scrutiny each time she'd circled the salon, and had managed to successfully ignore him.

'Francesca.'

He had the tread of a cat. Francesca turned slowly to face him. 'Dominic,' she acknowledged with due solemnity.

His smile was warm, and his eyes held amusement as he took hold of her hand and lifted it to his lips.

The touch was fleeting, yet she felt as if she'd been branded by fire. Heat flared through her veins, travelling a damning path. If he'd wanted to disconcert her, he'd succeeded.

Potent sexuality at its most lethal, she thought shakily. Wielded by an infinitely dangerous man who, unless she was mistaken, would play the game by his own rules.

He sensed the slight quiver of nervous awareness, felt the startled tightening of her fingers, and allowed her to pull free of him. For now.

During the past hour he'd watched her display a variety of clothes, admired her body's graceful movement, the tilt of her head, the warm generous smile.

Outwardly cool, she schooled her features into a polite mask, and knew that she hadn't fooled him in the slightest.

'If you'll excuse me?' She wanted, needed to get away.

'No.'

The refusal startled her. 'I beg your pardon?'

'No,' he repeated quietly.

Francesca pitched her voice sufficiently low so that no one else could hear. 'Just what the hell do you think you're doing?'

His gaze was steady. 'At this precise moment?'

She lifted one hand and let it fall to her side in angry resignation. 'OK, let's go with "this precise moment".'

A fleeting smile lightened his features, and she caught a glimpse of gleaming white teeth. 'Inviting you to lunch.'

Now it was her turn. 'No.'

His eyes gleamed with dark humour. 'I could add persuasion and kiss you in front of Margo's guests.'

Her voice lowered to a furious whisper. 'Do that, and I'll *hit* you.'

'It might be worth it to see you try.' He didn't give her time to think as he captured her face and lowered his head down to hers.

It wasn't a gentle touching of mouths, or a sensual tasting. Nor was it particularly brief.

This was claim-staking. Possession. Erotic, evocative, and intensely sexual.

Shock reverberated through her body, and she instinctively lifted her hands in an attempt to effect leverage against his chest.

He eased the pressure a little, and she tore her mouth away from his.

'You—'

He stilled the flow of angry words by placing a finger against her lips. 'Not here, unless you want to cause a scene.'

Her eyes sparked with fury, and her mouth shook as she sought to gain some measure of control. She became aware of her surroundings, the salon's occupants, and she wanted to verbally damn him as he took hold of her arm and led her outside.

'You arrogant, egotistical *fiend*,' Francesca accused the second they were alone.

'You didn't respond to my message, and with your telephone and mobile number ex-directory, your address unlisted, you left me no alternative.' He didn't add that he possessed sufficient influence to infiltrate the tight security screen she'd erected around her public and private persona.

'You inveigled an invitation to Margo's showing on that basis?' Anger was very much to the fore, sharpening the gold flecks in her eyes, accentuating the tilt of her head, stiffening her stance. She wanted to rage at him with a torrent of words that would singe the hair on his head.

He shrugged his shoulders. 'It was an interesting experience.'

'That's all you have to say?'

'It gave me the opportunity to watch you at work.'

Being one of few men in a room filled with avid women fashion-followers couldn't have held much appeal. 'I hope you suffered!'

Dark eyes gleamed, and his lips parted to form a quizzical smile. 'Oh, I did, believe me.'

Her chin lifted, and her eyes sparked furious fire.

'What is it with you? Do I present a challenge or something?'

Mockery was very much in evidence. 'Or something.'

It was a loaded statement, one that she refused to examine. 'Let me make it quite clear.' She drew in a deep breath. 'You're wasting your time.'

'That's a matter of opinion.'

Francesca closed her eyes, then opened them again. 'You know my father. Gabbi and Benedict Nicols are mutual friends.'

'What we share has nothing to do with your father, Gabbi or Benedict. Or anyone else for that matter.'

Emotion clouded her features, fleeting and pain-filled. 'We don't share *anything*.'

'Not yet,' Dominic said quietly. 'But we will.' He cupped her cheek in one hand and brushed his thumb along the length of her jaw. And didn't miss the movement in her throat as she compulsively swallowed.

Francesca glimpsed the deceptive indolence apparent in those deep eyes, the silent assurance of a man who knew what he wanted and would allow nothing to stand in his way. The knowledge tripped her pulse and made her heart beat faster. She had to put some distance between them.

'Please let me go.'

It was the 'please' that did it. He trailed his hand down her cheek, outlined her lips with the pad of one forefinger, then he dropped his hand down to his side as he offered a quizzical smile.

'I guess we don't get to eat together?'

'I have to be in the city in half an hour.' And lunch was going to be a salad sandwich and bottled water she'd pick up and eat along the way.

'Another modelling assignment?'

'A photographic shoot.' She took one step back, another to the side. 'I really must go.'

Francesca turned and crossed the road. She could feel a distinct prickle of awareness between her shoulderblades, and she was conscious of every step she took along the pavement.

It was only when she was safely behind the wheel of her car that the tension began to ease, and by the time she reached the city Dominic was firmly expelled from her mind.

The fashion shoot was exhausting, with the designer insisting the photographer do numerous takes from every conceivable angle. Accessories were changed countless times, her make-up touched and retouched, her hairstyle switched from loose and unruly to casually upswept, then confined in a sleek French pleat.

'Anything planned tonight, darling? I'd like to move outdoors, capture you on a lonely beach against the backdrop of a fading sunset.'

It was after six, and she was battling the onset of a headache. More than anything she wanted to step into her own clothes, climb into her car and drive back to her apartment. And sink into a spa and sip a long, cool drink, she added silently.

As a photographer, Tony was a perfectionist. And she was sufficiently professional to want to work *with* rather than against him.

'Are you going to allow me time to eat?' she queried with resignation.

'Of course, sweetie.' His smile was quick, and his eyes held a humorous gleam. 'I'm not an absolute monster.'

'Although you'll want me here early in the morning for dawn shots,' Francesca accorded with cynicism.

'How well you know me.' There was a certain wryness evident. 'But I'm the best.'

Knowledge, not vanity. He won awards every year for his photographic skill, and harboured a genuine love for the camera. Able to combine subject and background to maximum effect on celluloid, and an exceptional strategist, he loathed temperament, lauded professionalism and went to any length to achieve the look he wanted.

Together, they worked as a team, stowing clothes and equipment before adjourning to a nearby café for a meal eaten alfresco at a verandah table offering splendid views over a leafy green park.

Afterwards they headed north in a small convoy of vehicles to a designated cove where a makeshift tent was erected in which Francesca could change.

The cool breeze from the ocean whispered across her skin and lifted a few loose tendrils of hair as she moved at Tony's bidding, providing one pose after another as he clicked off rolls of film.

'Just a few more, Francesca. I want to do some black and white shots.'

Dusk began to dim the peripheral fringes, providing shadows that grew and lengthened, shading colour and merging lines.

'OK, that's it,' called Tony.

The equipment was dismantled, the clothes restored into individual garment bags and packed into the van. Lights along the boardwalk provided illumination, in direct contrast to the expanse of indigo sea.

Tony stowed his camera in the car, then turned towards her. 'Care to join me in a drink? There's a trendy little bar two blocks away.'

'Will you be offended if I say no?' Francesca countered.

'A date, darling?'

She smiled as they left the sand and stepped onto the bricked walk. 'With my bed. Solo,' she added as she anticipated his response. 'I imagine you'd prefer me bright-eyed and vivacious tomorrow?'

'As a photographer, yes,' he grinned. 'As a man, I'd derive pleasure from seeing you languorous and sated after a long night of loving.'

An arrow of pain lanced her body's core, and it cost a lot to inject a degree of humour into her voice and keep it light. 'You don't give up.'

'Maybe one of these days you'll say yes.'

He was a nice man. Personable, intelligent, and easy to talk to. She'd worked with him frequently in the past, and wanted to continue to work with him in the future.

'To a drink?'

His laughter brought a smile to her lips. 'Know all the angles, darling?'

'Almost every one,' she assured.

'So,' he concluded slowly, 'no shared nightcap, not even coffee?'

'I'm taking a raincheck, remember?' She leaned forward and placed a fleeting kiss to his cheek. '*Ciao*, Tony. I'll see you in the morning.'

CHAPTER FIVE

ELECTRONIC chimes brought Francesca into a state of wakefulness, and she uttered a faint groan as she rolled over to hit the 'stop' button.

Damn Tony and his photographic inspiration. Yet, even as she silently cursed him, she was sufficiently professional to recognise his vision. And doubtless she would applaud it when she sighted the finished prints.

A shower swept away any vestiges of the night's cobwebs, and a glass of fresh orange juice did much to revitalise her energy. It was too early for breakfast, so she merely extracted a banana from the bowl of fruit in the kitchen.

Attired in stylish loose-fitting cotton trousers and matching top, basic make-up complete, she slid her feet into low-heeled sandals, collected her bag, then took the lift down to the underground car park.

Within minutes she reached the main arterial road. Traffic at this early hour was minimal, and there was almost an eerie solitude in traversing darkened streets whose only illumination came from regulated electric lamps.

There was a tendency to be introspective and allow one's thoughts free passage.

Dominic Andrea. An intriguing man, with diverse interests and recognised as a skilled entrepreneur. There could be little doubt that that skill extended to the bedroom...or wherever else he chose to indulge in sex.

She drew the line at defining it as lovemaking. 'Love' was a definitive word that had little to do with a mutual slaking of the senses as two people took pleasure in each other's body without trust or commitment.

The thought of Dominic Andrea in the role of lover aroused feelings she found difficult to dispel. To tread such a path would be madness.

Dear heaven, what was the matter with her?

Francesca reached forward and switched on the car radio, grateful for the busy sound of rock music and the artificial brightness of an early morning DJ. It helped redirect her focus.

Which, she rationalised, was a dawn fashion shoot that needed to be set up in early-morning darkness with everything in readiness for the first sign of light on the horizon.

Three cars and a van hugged the kerb when she slid to a halt behind Tony's distinctive BMW. Lights were already set up on the beach, the tent was in position, and as she drew close she could hear the sound of muted voices.

'Morning, everyone.'

Tony gave her a weary smile as she entered the tent. 'Good girl, you're on time.' He cast his watch a quick glance. 'Ten minutes, OK? Same gown, hairstyle. Less make-up.'

The sky was just beginning to lighten as Francesca assumed position within a metre of the receding tide. Wet sand gleamed like well-oiled gunmetal, melding with a smooth liquid sea.

Before their eyes grey shadows melted beneath the emergence of soft colour, like the transforming brush from an artist's palette. And the air bore a freshness untouched by the sun's warmth.

'Let's get this show on the road. We won't have long,' Tony warned as he lifted his camera. 'Francesca?'

'Ready when you are.'

The camera clicked, shutter moving forward as he called for her to move this way, then that.

'Head up a little higher. That's it. Hold it. Now turn towards me and smile. Mona Lisa, darling.' Shot after shot was taken. 'OK, now we want happy. Not quite laughing. Got it.'

The shutter whirred at a fast pace. 'Movement, sweetie,' he directed. 'Let's see that skirt swirl, shall we? More. Again. And again.' He was moving rapidly, his hands and body co-ordinating perfectly as he talked. 'Damn. The light's coming up fast.'

Five minutes later he capped the lens. 'That should do it. Thanks, everyone.'

It was shaping up to be a hectic day, Francesca perceived a trifle ruefully as she shed the gown, then pulled on her trousers and top. At lunch she was booked to tread another catwalk, and this evening she was due to dine at her father's home. With deft movements she twisted her hair into a knot atop her head, then slid her feet into sandals.

'Care to share coffee before we each get on with the day?' Tony queried as she emerged from the tent.

'Love to,' Francesca accepted, grateful for their

easy friendship as they trod a path across the sand to the parked cars.

They each stowed their bags, locked the boot, then crossed the road to the beachside café.

'I'll order,' Tony indicated as they slid into an empty booth. 'Short black?'

'Please,' she responded gratefully, and sipped the dark aromatic brew from the cup placed in front of her shortly afterwards.

'You're covering today's charity luncheon at the Hilton?'

''fraid so, darling.' He drained his cup and signalled for the waitress to refill it.

'All those dowagers dressed to kill, fawning over you in a bid to have their photo appear in the society pages, huh?' Francesca teased, and caught his faint grimace.

'They send me gifts. Champagne, expensive trinkets. One matron even went so far as to offer an unforgettable all-expenses-paid weekend on Hayman Island.'

'Tell me you declined.'

He offered a wry smile. 'I don't accept bribes, as tempting as some appear.'

It was almost eight when Francesca slid behind the wheel of her car and drove to the gym. An exercise routine was so much a part of her daily regime that she scarcely gave it a thought.

There was little time to spare when she returned to her apartment in order to shower, dress, and drive into the city.

The fundraising luncheon in aid of the Australian Cancer Society was a major event. The venue was prestigious, and the guest list read like an excerpt from the city's register of the city's rich and famous.

'Sell-out' was whispered from one to the other as the speeches progressed and lunch was served. Then the compère announced the start of the fashion parade and the music began.

The main lights dimmed and strategically aimed arc lights lit the catwalk. Showtime.

Afterwards, Francesca tidied her hair, retouched her make-up, then collected her bag. With luck she'd be able to slip out and make an exit without too much delay.

She was halfway across the room when she heard a familiar voice call her name.

'*Francesca.*'

Her stepmother, with Katherine at her side, seated at a nearby table. 'You'll join us for a coffee, won't you?'

Madeline was adept at making a query sound like a command, and there was little Francesca could do other than slip into the indicated seat.

Katherine offered a conspiratorial wink, well aware that her mother's main purpose in issuing the invitation was to bolster her own social prestige. Smart girl, Katherine.

It was thirty minutes before Francesca could orchestrate her escape, and a further half an hour before she joined the flow of traffic leaving the city. Consequently it was almost five when she re-entered her apartment.

After a day exchanging one elegant outfit for another, she would have preferred to slip on a robe,

eat a light chicken salad, watch television, then settle for an early night.

Instead, she selected a stunning black silk trouser
suit, added a touch of gold jewellery, applied minimum make-up, highlighted her eyes, and left her
hair loose to cascade onto her shoulders.

Lights blazed in welcome as Francesca traversed
the long, curved driveway leading to Rick and
Madeline's elegant double-storeyed Tudor-style
home situated high in suburban Vaucluse.

The interior reflected Madeline's exquisite taste,
and Francesca greeted Katherine and John with affection, brushed cheeks with her stepmother and accepted Rick's warm bear-hug.

'Have a seat, Francesca,' Madeline bade. 'Rick
will get you a drink.'

Diplomacy and an adeptness born of many years'
experience in recognising Madeline's *modus oper-
andi* ensured that Francesca kept within the un-
written boundaries. Once you knew the game, it
was relatively easy to play.

'Orange juice? A wine spritzer?'

'A spritzer would be great,' she accepted
warmly.

The sound of the door chimes provided an inter-
ruption, and Madeline turned towards Rick. 'That
will be Dominic. Let him in, darling.' She turned
to Francesca. 'You don't mind the inclusion of another guest?'

There was nothing she could do except smile. 'Of
course not.'

Rick knew better than to matchmake. Madeline,
however, had no such qualms, and was adept at

assembling people together in order to create an interesting evening.

Dominic Andrea's motives for accepting the invitation were open to conjecture.

'He's really a hunk, isn't he?' Katherine enthused with teenage fervour, and Francesca was saved from making comment as her father ushered Dominic into the lounge.

In her line of business she came into contact with many visually attractive men, but few possessed this man's aura of power. It went beyond the physical, and meshed with a dangerous sexuality that threatened a woman's equilibrium. A potent combination, she conceded as she took in his expensive suit, silk tie, hand-stitched shoes, before allowing her gaze to settle on those broad, chiselled features.

Generous mouth, cleaved from a sensual mould. Eyes so dark, yet as expressive as he chose them to be. At this precise moment there was a tinge of humour beneath the projected warmth.

'Madeline.' He moved forward with fluid grace, took hold of his hostess's hand, then turned towards her stepdaughter.

'Francesca.'

'Dominic,' she acknowledged coolly. She felt on edge already, and he'd only just entered the room. What on earth would she be like at the end of the evening?

Unsettled, if he had anything to do with it.

'A drink, Dominic?' Rick was a considerate host who kept a well-stocked liquor cabinet designed to cater to the whim of any guest.

'Thanks. A soda.'

Madeline smiled. 'The need for a clear head?'

'Perhaps Dominic has an ulcer,' Francesca offered sweetly. 'I imagine an artistic temperament and the pressure of business play havoc with the stress levels.'

'Not an inclination to minimise alcohol to one glass of wine with the evening meal?'

She tilted her head and viewed him in silence for several long seconds. 'How.' She paused deliberately. 'Boring.'

His mouth curved slightly. 'You prefer a man whose mind and actions are clouded with alcohol?'

Oh, my. Was she the only one present who picked up on that *double entendre*?

Francesca silently willed the evening to pass quickly so that she could make her escape at the soonest possible moment without causing Madeline or her father offence.

She caught Dominic's faintly raised eyebrow, and realised that he'd accurately assessed her thoughts.

'I had no idea you were joining us tonight.' As a conversational gambit, it lacked inspiration.

His eyes held hidden warmth and a degree of cynical humour. 'Madeline issued an invitation to look at the positioning of two of my paintings in her home.'

Her head tilted fractionally. 'Do you make it a practice to approve where your paintings hang in all your buyers' homes?'

'Rarely,' he conceded.

'Rick and Madeline should feel duly honoured.'

His soft laughter was unexpected, the humour

tilting the curve of his mouth and fanning tiny lines from each corner of his eyes. Eyes that were remarkably steady, even watchful as he caught each fleeting expression on her finely boned features.

'Perhaps.' Dominic lifted a hand and tucked a stray tendril of hair behind her ear in a gesture deliberately designed to startle. 'Although let there be no doubt that the main reason I'm here tonight is *you.*'

He glimpsed the faint widening of her eyes, the momentary shock, before she successfully masked her expression.

'Dinner is served, ma'am.' The cook's intrusion was a timely one, and Francesca expelled a relieved sigh as Madeline led the way.

Seating was arranged with Madeline and Rick facing each other at the head of the table, Katherine and John on one side, with Dominic and Francesca seated together.

Vichyssoise was followed by barbecued prawns on a bed of rice, with steamed fish, hollandaise sauce and salad as a main course. Crème caramel and fresh fruit sufficed as dessert.

A pleasant meal in what would have been relaxing company—if it hadn't been for Dominic's presence. Francesca was acutely aware of his every action, the smell of clean tailoring mingling with the subtle tones of his exclusive cologne.

He used his cutlery with precise, decisive movements, his enjoyment of the food evident, and he skilfully drew Katherine and John into the conversation, transforming John into an amusing raconteur while Katherine bloomed beneath his attention.

Madeline was at her best. Fame or fortune in a guest was a bonus. To have two dine at her table who could lay claim to both was a considerable *coup*. Rick, sensing his wife's satisfaction, became more expansive as the evening progressed.

'Shall we adjourn to the lounge for coffee?' Madeline queried, signalling just that intention by standing to her feet.

Everyone followed her directive, but Francesca was unprepared when Dominic moved behind her and drew out her chair.

She hadn't expected the courtesy, didn't want it, and had to consciously refrain from pulling her arm away as his fingers lightly clasped her elbow.

'Katherine, John,' Madeline invited graciously. 'If you choose, you can retire upstairs and view television.'

An exemplary mother, and a very shrewd one. Political correctness and good manners were something Madeline insisted upon. It said much that neither of her children grasped the excuse to leave.

Fifteen minutes max, Francesca decided, then she would express her thanks and depart. She sank gracefully into a lounge chair and accepted coffee.

It had been a long day, and tomorrow, after seeing her mother, she'd agreed to join a panel of judges assembled to select three junior models from twenty young hopefuls parading their stuff on the catwalk.

Friday, Saturday and Sunday were free, and she'd designated them as *hers*. For pampering, a professional haircut, a massage. Sheer indulgence.

Unbidden, her eyes met those of Dominic, and

she glimpsed the degree of sensual warmth evident in those dark depths. He presented a disturbing factor, and she was in no doubt of the steel-willed determination beneath the surface.

Francesca finished her coffee, declined a refill, and rose to her feet. 'If you'll excuse me, I really must leave.' Her warm smile encompassed Rick, Madeline, Katherine and John. 'It's been a lovely evening.'

'Likewise,' Dominic accorded with ease as he unwound his length from the chair. 'It's been very enjoyable.'

Why was he timing his departure to coincide with her own? Why shouldn't he? a silent voice demanded as she crossed the lounge at Rick's side, brushed a quick kiss to his cheek at the front door, then stepped quickly down the steps.

'Running away?' Dominic's voice held slight amusement as he matched his pace to her own.

She withdrew a keyring from her evening purse in readiness, and walked past a black Lexus to where her own car was parked. She selected a key and inserted it into the door.

His arm brushed hers as he reached forward and undid the latch, then drew open the door.

'How was your day?'

She slipped past him and slid into the driver's seat. 'You can't really want to know.'

He placed an arm on the roof and leaned in towards her. 'Yes. Humour me, Francesca.'

She slid the safety belt across and clipped it into position. She should have felt in control, yet somehow the advantage appeared to be his.

'A three-thirty a.m. start for a dawn photographic shoot, a fashion parade at the Hilton, dinner with family.'

'And guest.'

'Unexpected guest,' she amended.

'Whom you would have preferred not to be present.'

She tilted her head in order to meet his gaze. 'Perhaps you'll enlighten me as to how you came by the invitation.'

'I occasionally do business with your father.' His shoulders shifted in a slight shrugging gesture. 'Madeline appears to appreciate my paintings. It wasn't difficult to make a phone call.'

No, she supposed. Not difficult at all for a skilful manipulator to pose a few pertinent questions within a conversation in order to gain his objective.

She looked at him carefully, and his sloping smile had the strangest effect, causing sensation to unfurl deep inside and creep insidiously through her body.

'What should I expect next?' She kept her voice deliberately cool. 'The "Your place or mine?" spiel?'

Dominic regarded her steadily. 'Interpreted as, "Let's get between the sheets and I'll show you what you're missing"? I don't play that particular game.'

'With any woman?'

'With you,' he declared with soft emphasis. He reached forward and caught hold of her chin between thumb and forefinger. 'Now, shall we begin again? Tomorrow—'

'There isn't going to be a tomorrow.' Her voice sounded thick and vaguely husky.

'Yes,' he said quietly. 'There is. The day after, or the one after that. Next week. Whenever.'

Francesca looked at him long and hard, saw the calm awareness in his eyes, and felt *exposed* in a way she'd never experienced before. Fear, apprehension—both were prevalent. And a strange sense of recognition. Almost as if something deep inside her had sought and found the matching half of a whole.

She didn't want to deal with it, with *him*, and what he represented. She wanted time to think, to evaluate. Saying yes to this man, on any level, would lead her towards a path she was hesitant to tread.

'This is one situation where your persistence won't pay off,' she assured him.

'You don't think so?'

'I know so.'

'Then prove me wrong and share lunch with me. Nominate a day.' A challenge. Would she accept or refuse?

Fine, she accorded a trifle grimly. If that was what it took to convince him she wasn't interested, she'd agree. Besides, lunch sounded *safe*. Broad daylight, with the excuse of work as a legitimate escape route.

Francesca gave him a long, level look. 'Friday,' she capitulated. 'Name the restaurant, and I'll meet you there.'

'Claude's, Oxford Street, Woollahra. One,' he said without missing a beat.

A fashionably chic French eating place where advance bookings were a must. 'Fine.' She slid the key into the ignition and fired the engine, watching as he stood back and closed the door.

Seconds later she cleared the gates and entered the wide, tree-lined suburban street, following it down until it joined with New South Head Road.

Electric streetlights shared a pattern uniformity, vying with colourful flashing neon signs illuminating the city's centre. Ferries traversed the dark waters of Port Jackson, and a large cruise ship was ablaze with light and life as a tugboat led it slowly towards the inner harbour.

Magical, Francesca reflected silently, and felt a strange pull towards another harbour in another city on the opposite side of the world. Another car, a Ferrari Testarossa, driven by Mario through the steep winding hills above Rome. And how she'd delighted at the sight spread out before her, laughed with the joy of life, then gasped at the speed with which Mario had driven home in order to make love with her.

Mad, halcyon days that couldn't last. Even then she'd been afraid the candle that burned so brightly within him was destined for a short life.

It was almost eleven when she garaged her car and took the lift up to her apartment. With care she shed her clothes, removed her make-up, then she donned a slither of silk and slid in between cool percale sheets.

CHAPTER SIX

AN ELEGANT woman, Sophy adored being *seen*. Consequently her choice of venue was one of the city's currently trendiest meeting places in town.

'*Drinks*, darling,' Sophy had specified the get-together, and Francesca slid into a reserved chair and ordered coffee.

Her mother would be late. After all these years it was accepted Sophy had no sense of time. Excuses, many and varied, were floated out with an airy wave of the hand, and her family and friends inevitably forgave her the lapse.

Thirty minutes wasn't too bad, Francesca conceeded wryly as she glimpsed her mother making an entrance. There had been occasions when she'd waited for up to an hour.

Titian hair styled in a shoulder-length bob, exquisite features, and slim curves a woman half her age would die for. Add an exclusive designer outfit, and Sophy presented a visual image that drew appreciative admiration.

'Sorry, sweetheart.' Sophy effected a careless shrug as she slid into the seat opposite. 'Armand...' Her mouth tilted wickedly. 'You know how it is. The French—everything is *l'amour*.'

'I thought you were through with Frenchmen,' Francesca said equably.

'Ah, but they are so *gallant*.' Sophy cast her

daughter an impish smile. 'Besides, darling, he is fantastic in bed.'

'How nice.'

'Yes,' her mother agreed, and her eyes gleamed with humour. 'It's a lovely bonus.'

Francesca wondered with philosophical resignation if Armand was even more unsuitable than his illustrious predecessor, who had squired her mother for a record ten months before Sophy discarded him.

'Now, sweetheart. Tell me what you think of your father. The last time I saw him I thought he was looking quite...' Sophy paused, then added delicately, 'Mature. A few more lines. I recommended my cosmetic surgeon, but you can imagine your father's response.'

Indeed. Voluble, to say the least.

'Madeline makes so many demands, and of course there's the children.'

An emotional minefield Francesca had no intention of entering. 'Would you like coffee?'

'Please.' Her eyes sharpened fractionally. 'You look—different.' Speculative interest was evident. 'Yes. Definitely.' Her mouth curved. 'It's a man, isn't it?'

A man. It seemed such a tame description for someone of Dominic Andrea's calibre.

'Now why would you think that?' Francesca countered evenly, and her mother smiled.

'Am I right?'

'Not really.'

'Ah,' Sophy declared with ambiguous satisfaction, and changed the subject. 'You have yet to mention Mario's mother. So sad. There was a nurse, of course?'

'Yes, round the clock.' Francesca didn't add that she'd shared each shift and snatched sleep as and when she could.

Frequenting the trendiest café ensured there were interruptions, as first one, then another of Sophy's friends stopped by. Introductions rarely identified Francesca as Sophy's *daughter*. Age was something her mother guarded jealously and refused to acknowledge to anyone—for how did a woman who *looked* thirty admit to a twenty-five-year-old progeny.

Armand duly arrived to collect his *amour*, and Francesca wondered how her mother could not see that the man was too attentive, too smooth, and too intent on feeding not only Sophy's ego but his own.

However, Francesca had long given up worrying about her mother's succession of paramours. Sophy was aware of all the angles.

The day after...next week...whenever. Dominic's words echoed inside Francesca's head as she considered calling him to say she'd changed her mind about meeting him.

Except she had the feeling all that would do was postpone the inevitable.

Perhaps it would be better to get it over and done with. They'd talk, eat, and discover whatever he thought they had in common didn't exist. And pigs might fly, she denounced disparagingly.

What existed between them was primeval chemistry, pure and simple. The question was, what was she going to do about it? More pertinently, what was she going to allow Dominic to do about it?

Oh, for heaven's sake. What are you afraid of? she silently berated herself.

Good question, Francesca noted wryly as she entered Claude's and was greeted by the *maître d'*.

'Ah, yes. Mr Andrea is already here.' His smile charmed, as it was meant to do. 'Please. Follow me.'

It was crazy to feel nervous. *Act*, a tiny voice prompted. You're good at it.

Dominic watched as she threaded her way through the room. He observed the number of heads turn in her direction, witnessed the speculation and admiration, and felt a certain empathy for their appreciation of Francesca's beauty.

Experience had taught him that the packaging didn't always reflect what existed in the heart, the mind, the soul, and that physical lust was an unsatisfactory entity without love. Consequently, he refused to settle for anything less.

As she drew close he sensed the imperceptible degree of nervousness beneath the sophisticated veneer, and discovered it pleased him.

He rose to his feet as she reached his table. 'Francesca.'

Her response was polite, and he smiled, aware of the defence mechanism firmly in place...and wondered how long it would take to demolish it.

The *maître d'* held out a chair and she sank into it. 'Madame would prefer a few minutes before she orders a drink?'

'I'll have an orange juice.'

'I shall inform the drink steward,' he said gravely, and with a snap of his fingers a formally clad waiter appeared out of nowhere, took her order, then disappeared.

The lighting was low, the tables small. And Dominic seemed much too close.

Francesca looked at him carefully, and his features seemed more finely chiselled, the bone structure more pronounced in the dim illumination. Dark hair, dark eyes, dark suit. It accentuated his breadth of shoulder and emphasised a physical fitness most men would aspire to.

A complex man, she decided instinctively, who was capable of savagery and great tenderness. It was evident in his painting, for he possessed hands that could slash bold colour on a canvas yet brush strokes on another with such sensitivity the contrast was vast—too vast to imagine the artists were one and the same.

And as a man, a lover? Was he wild and untamed? Sensitive and loving? Were his emotions always under control? *Did she want them to be?*

Oh, God, where had that come from?

With a sense of desperation she picked up the menu and began to peruse it.

'If I say you look beautiful, will you hold it against me?'

His voice held mild amusement, and she lowered the menu, cast him a level look, then offered him a singularly sweet smile.

'Probably.'

A soft chuckle escaped from his throat. 'Should

we aim for polite conversation, or opt for companionable silence?'

'You could tell me what you did yesterday, then I'll tell you what I did,' she said with marked solemnity. 'That should take care of ten minutes or so.'

'Yesterday? I caught an early-morning flight to Melbourne, attended a meeting, lunched with a business associate, flew back mid-afternoon, and played squash.'

'You were meant to stretch that out a bit, not condense it into thirty seconds.'

He reached for his wine glass, lifted it, sipped from the contents, then replaced it onto the table. 'And you?'

'Sat on a panel judging junior models, caught up with my mother.'

'And thought of any number of reasons why you should cancel lunch today?'

It was a stab in the dark, but an accurate one. She opted to go with honesty. 'Yes.'

One eyebrow slanted. 'Do I pose such a threat?'

'You unnerve me.' The words slipped out without thought.

'That's a plus,' Dominic drawled.

She decided to set a few boundaries. 'We're sharing lunch. Nothing more.'

'For now,' he qualified. 'Shall we order? I can recommend the escargots.'

It was an acquired taste, but one she favoured.

The waiter appeared, noted their selection, and disappeared.

Francesca lifted her glass and took a long sip of

iced water, then set the glass carefully on the table. Her eyes met his, their expression wary, faintly wry.

'Do you have anything planned for the weekend?' Dominic queried, and she rested the fork onto her plate then took time to dab her mouth with the napkin before answering.

'A quiet few days—no family, no social engagements.'

'Time out?'

Her fingers strayed to toy with the stem of her drinking glass. 'Yes.'

'There's a function in one of the major city hotels tomorrow evening for which I have tickets. Gabbi and Benedict suggest we join their table.'

Gabbi was a dear friend, whose company she enjoyed. Dominic was something else entirely. The thought that he had no willing partner he could call upon was ludicrous.

'I lend my support to a few charities, but rarely attend their social functions.'

Was her expression so easily readable? She wouldn't have thought so, yet this man possessed an uncanny ability to read her mind.

'Then why are you attending this particular one?'

He leaned back in his chair and regarded her with studied ease. 'Because it provides me with an opportunity to ask you out.'

'And no doubt you meant to sweeten the invitation by joining up with two of my best friends?'

The waiter cleared their plates, and inclined his head as they declined dessert and settled for coffee.

'A simple yes or no will do,' Dominic mocked, and she gave him a brilliant smile.

He always seemed to be one step ahead of her, and for once she felt inclined to reverse the process by doing the unexpected. 'Yes.'

He didn't display so much as a flicker of surprise, nor did he indicate satisfaction at her answer. 'Let me have your address and I'll collect you.'

She wanted to protest, acknowledged the foolishness of taking independence too far, then gave it, watching idly as he penned the apartment number and street on the back of a card.

It was after two when they emerged from the restaurant.

'Where are you parked?'

Francesca felt the touch of his hand on her arm and wanted to pull away, yet stay. A true contradiction in terms, she acknowledged wryly as she fought the deep, curling sensation that slowly unfurled and began spreading through her body.

'About fifty metres to the left.'

It was mid-afternoon and there were several people within close proximity. So why did she feel *threatened*? Fanciful thinking, she dismissed, and resisted the inclination to dismiss *him*, here, now, and walk quickly to her car.

Minutes later she paused at the kerb and withdrew her car keys.

He seemed to loom large, his height and breadth intimidating, and the breath caught in her throat as his head lowered down to hers.

A kiss, brief, in farewell. She would accept the

firm brush of his lips, then step back and smile, slip into her car and drive away.

Francesca wasn't prepared for the warm softness of a mouth that seemed far too attuned to her own, its wants and needs.

Unbidden, her hands crept up to tangle together at his nape as he pulled her close, and a soft protest rose and died in her throat as he deepened the kiss to something so intimate, her whole body flamed with an answering fire.

An invasion of the senses, exploring, savouring. He conquered in a manner that made her forget who she was, and where.

When he lifted his head she felt lost, almost adrift, for the few seconds it took for her to regain a sense of reality.

Her eyes were wide and luminous, and she felt a sense of shock. And shame.

'Tomorrow,' Dominic reminded her gently. 'Six-thirty.' His smile was warm. 'Drive carefully.'

He wasn't even breathing quickly, whereas she felt as if she'd just been tossed high by an errant wave and carried breathless and choking into shore.

She didn't say a word. Couldn't, she rationalised as she stepped from the kerb and crossed round the car to unlock her door.

With every semblance of calm, she started the engine, reversed the necessary metre to allow her clear passage into the flow of traffic, then moved the car out onto the road.

It wasn't until she was several kilometres distant that she began to breathe normally, and later that night, as she lay sleepless in bed, she could still feel the possession of his mouth on her own, the imprint of his body against hers, and the intoxication of her senses.

Francesca woke early, and after a leisurely breakfast she showered and dressed, then drove to a Double Bay clinic for her scheduled massage, facial and manicure.

Lunch was followed by a leisurely browse through several boutiques. One outfit really impressed her, together with shoes and matching bag. Her experienced eye put them all together and transposed them onto her stepsister's slender frame, and she smiled with pleasure as she anticipated Katherine's reaction when she received the gift.

There was time for a coffee with Margo, and it was after four when she slid into the car and headed home. The sun was strong, and she automatically reached for her sunglasses, only to discover they weren't atop her head. They weren't in her bag, either, and she cursed beneath her breath at the thought of having misplaced them.

Sensitivity to strong sunlight occasionally triggered a migraine, particularly if she was under stress, and it was a situation she took precautions to avoid.

By the time she reached her apartment block the familiar ache had begun behind her right eye. If she was lucky, ordinary painkillers would arrest it, otherwise prescription pills and several hours' rest were the only source of relief.

Francesca gave it half an hour, then she rum-

maged in her bag for Dominic's card and reached
for the phone.

He answered his mobile on the third ring. 'Andrea.'

The sound of his voice increased the splintering
pain in her head. It hurt to talk, and she kept it as
brief as possible.

'I'm in the vicinity of Double Bay. I'll be there
within minutes.'

'No, don't—' It was too late, he'd already cut
the call.

She didn't want him here. She didn't want anyone here. Even thinking hurt, so she didn't even try
to qualify anything, she simply retrieved the packet
of prescription pills and took the required dosage.

When the in-house phone buzzed she answered
it, then pressed the release button as Dominic identified himself.

Francesca was waiting at the door when he came
out of the lift, and he took one look at her pale
face, the dark bruised eyes, then gently pushed her
inside the lounge and closed the door.

'That bad, hmm?' He brushed his lips to her temple. 'You've taken medication? OK, let's get you
into bed.'

She struggled between comfort and propriety.
'The couch.' Her protest was less than a whisper,
for it would be heaven to rest her head against his
chest and close her eyes.

Ignoring her, he put an arm beneath her knees,
lifted her into his arms, and took a calculated guess
as to which room was hers.

The bedroom was much as he had imagined it

would be. Feminine, but not overly so. There were no frills, no clutter on flat surfaces, and the colour scheme was pale peach and green.

Without a word he closed the drapes, folded back the bedcovers, then, ignoring her protest, he carefully removed her outer clothes and gently deposited her onto the bed.

'Comfortable?'

The medication was allowing her to sink into numbing, almost pain-free oblivion. 'Yes.'

Dominic drew the sheet up to her shoulders then sank into a nearby *chaise*, his expression enigmatic as he watched her breathing deepen.

Unless he was mistaken, she'd sleep through until the early-morning hours. He'd stay for a while, then he'd leave.

She looked peaceful. Her features in repose bore a classic beauty, the facial bone structure in perfect symmetry, alabaster skin as soft and smooth as silk. And a generous mouth that could tilt with laughter and curve with sensual promise.

Yet there was a vulnerability evident he knew she would just hate anyone—him especially—to witness. An inner fragility that tugged at something deep inside him and made him feel immensely protective.

Dammit, he wanted the right to be part of her life. To earn her respect, her trust. And her love. The *forever* kind. Commitment. *Marriage*.

After one union that had ended tragically, it wasn't going to be an easy task to persuade her to marry again. Nor would she readily believe it was *love* he felt for her, not merely physical lust.

The temptation to cancel out of tonight and be here when she woke was strong. However, she'd resent such vigilance rather than thank him for it.

He left quietly, secured the door, then took the lift down to the lobby and drove home.

It was dark when Francesca stirred, and she opened her eyes long enough to determine she was in bed, then she closed them again, drifting easily back to sleep.

The sun was filtering through the drapes, lightening the room when she woke again, and she groaned as she glanced at the bedside clock.

Food. And something to drink. She tossed the sheet aside, slid to her feet, then padded into the kitchen.

A glass of fresh orange juice did much to begin the revitalising process, and she switched on the coffeemaker, slid bread into the toaster, and nibbled a banana while she waited. Cereal, a hardboiled egg, toast and an apple ought to do it, she mused as the coffee began to filter. Toast popped up, and when the coffee was ready she sank onto a high stool and took the first appreciative sip of caffeine. Bliss. Absolute bliss.

When she'd finished eating she'd take a leisurely shower, then dress and decide what to do with the day.

Meanwhile, she reflected on Dominic's ministrations, and his presence in her bedroom before the medication had taken its full effect. How long had he stayed? And *why*? She wasn't sure if she wanted to know the answer.

The phone rang twice while she was in the shower, and when she checked the answering machine the first call was from Dominic, the second from Gabbi.

She dialled Gabbi's number first, and apologised for her absence the previous night.

Gabbi's voice was full of concern. 'Are you sure you're OK?'

'Fully recovered and ready to face the day,' she reassured her. 'How were things last night?'

There was a momentary pause. 'It was a sell-out. Dinner was fine, and everyone declared the fashion parade to be a huge success.'

'You're hedging, Gabbi. I take it Annaliese played up?'

'You could say that.'

'Much as it goes against the grain, I think you're going to have to get down and dirty with that young lady.'

'Ah, now there's a thought. Any suggestions?'

'Yell? Throw something?'

'All out war, Francesca?' There was amusement evident. 'Think of the repercussions.'

Francesca wrinkled her nose. 'Benedict wouldn't give a damn.'

'Annaliese and her mother are a formidable pair,' Gabbi responded soberly.

Indeed. Francesca considered herself fortunate her own step-siblings were of the loving kind. And Madeline, although fiercely territorial, wasn't sufficiently vindictive to deliberately drive a wedge between Rick and his daughter.

'I suggest you sharpen your claws,' Francesca

indicated with a touch of wry humour, and heard Gabbi's laugh echo down the line.

'Filed and ready.'

They ended the call on a light note, and Francesca was about to punch in the digits to connect with Dominic's mobile when the phone rang.

'Francesca.' Her pulse quickened and went into overdrive at the sound of Dominic's voice. 'You slept well?'

'Yes. Thank you,' she added politely.

'For what, precisely?'

His indolent query raised goosebumps where goosebumps had no right to be. Why was she thanking him? For caring enough to be there for her? Ensuring she was comfortably settled and waiting until the medication took effect? 'Just— thank you.'

She could almost see his features relaxing with a degree of humour, and that sensuously moulded mouth curve into a smile.

'Want to join me on a picnic?'

The question startled her, and she hesitated, torn by an image of finger food eaten alfresco.

'If I refuse, will you seclude yourself in the studio and paint?'

He gave a husky laugh. 'Something like that.'

There was a pull of the senses she found difficult to ignore, and she aimed for a light response. 'How about a compromise?'

'Shoot.'

'I'll come watch you paint, *then* we go on a picnic.'

'You just want to see my etchings.'

She couldn't help the smile that curved the edges of her mouth. 'You've seen *me* at work.'

'Much more glamorous than a pile of blank canvas, numerous quantities of oil paint and mineral turps, I can assure you.'

'We have a deal?'

'Deal,' he responded easily.

'Give me five minutes and I'll be on my way.'

She retrieved a spare pair of sunglasses from the bedroom and slipped them into her bag. Should she contribute some food? Her refrigerator wasn't exactly a receptacle of gourmet treats. Fruit and frozen bread did not a feast make. OK, so she'd stop off somewhere *en route* and collect a few things.

Which was precisely what she did, arriving at Dominic's front door with no less than two carry-bags held in each hand.

'I invited you to join me on a picnic, not provide one,' he remonstrated as he divested her of her purchases.

'I got carried away. Besides, I owe you a meal.'

'You don't owe me anything.'

She followed him through to the kitchen. 'Humour me. I have an independent streak.'

A friendly room with modern appliances, she decided as he unpacked the bags and stored a cold-pack in the refrigerator.

She cast him an all-encompassing look, appraising the sleeveless shirt, the cut-off jeans, the trainers on his feet.

One eyebrow slanted. 'What did you expect? An enveloping artist's cape?' His eyes gleamed as he reached out a hand and touched one cheek, glimpsed the faint uncertainty evident and sought to alleviate it. 'Shall we go?'

She didn't resist as he led her to the glassed walkway, connecting the large studio above a multi-car garage to the house.

It was, she conceded, an artist's dream, with sections of floor-to-ceiling glass and sliding floor-to-ceiling cupboard doors closing storage areas. Even the roof held panels of glass to capture every angle of sunlight.

There were the tools of trade in evidence—pots and tubes of oil paint, three easels, canvas, frames—all tidily stored on racks.

Yet she saw splotches of paint on the bare wooden floor, denoting it as a functional room where work was achieved.

'Do you need to paint in silence? Or doesn't noise bother you?'

'Depends on the mood, and the creative muse,' Dominic answered, watching her closely. This was his sanctum, a room which revealed more of himself than he liked. Consequently he allowed very few people access.

'Tell me where you'd prefer me to sit or stand while you paint.'

'You don't want to explore?'

'I imagine if there's something you want to show me, you will,' Francesca said evenly.

'Take a seat, while I create a colourful abstract to be auctioned off for charity next week.'

She watched him turn a blank canvas into a visual work of art. First the block of colour, covered by bold strokes and strong slashes. It looked so easy, his movements sure as one hour passed, then another, and she sat there enthralled by his artistic ability to transfer image to canvas. It didn't seem to matter that she possessed little comprehension of the portrayed abstract or its symmetry. The creative process itself was inspiring.

His involvement was total, and interest, rather than curiosity, impelled a strong desire to see some of his completed works. She would have given much to examine the tiered rack where several canvases were stored. Maybe next time.

At last he stood back satisfied. 'That's enough for today.' He deftly deposited brushes, cleaned paint from his hands, then crossed to a nearby sink and washed.

'Let's get out of here.'

He left her in the kitchen. 'I'll go shower and change while you pack food into the cooler.'

He reappeared ten minutes later, dressed in casual trousers and a short-sleeved polo shirt.

They drove north to a delightful inlet that was relatively isolated.

'Hungry?' Dominic queried as he spread a rug on a grassy bank overlooking a curved half moon of sand and sea.

It was almost mid-afternoon. 'Famished.'

Francesca began unpacking the cooler while he unfurled a large beach umbrella and staked it firmly into the ground to provide essential shade.

She set out plates, fresh bread rolls, sliced ham, chicken and salads, brie, fruit.

'A soda?'

'Please,' she accepted gratefully, uncapping the bottle and taking a long swallow of iced liquid.

Dominic split the bread rolls in half and began filling them, then handed her one. 'OK?'

She took a bite, then grinned. 'Excellent.' She felt relaxed, despite the intimacy of their solitude. Carefree, she realized. Something she hadn't experienced in a long time.

Deep down she knew she should be wary, on guard against the mood between them taking a subtle shift. As it inevitably would. But not today. Today she needed some light-hearted fun, and the opportunity to get to know Dominic Andrea, the man beneath the projected persona.

'Tell me about yourself.'

He finished one bread roll and filled another. The look he directed her was piercing, steady. 'What do you want to know?'

'Where you were born, family.'

'The personal profile?' he mocked gently. 'Athens. My parents emigrated to Australia when I was seven. I have two younger sisters, one lives in America, the other in Santorini. My mother returned there five years ago when my father died from a heart attack.'

'Do you see them often?'

His smile held amusement. 'Every year.'

Somehow she'd pictured him as self-sufficient and a loner. 'I guess you have nieces, nephews?'

'Two of each, aged from three months to six years.'

It wasn't difficult to imagine him hoisting a squealing child astride his shoulders, or playing ball. Why hadn't he married and begun a family of his own?

'How about you?'

It was a fair question, and one she sought to answer with equal brevity. 'Sydney-born and educated. Two step-siblings on my father's side. Several from my mother's numerous marriages.'

She wasn't willing to provide him with any more facts than he already knew. 'Let's walk along the beach.'

She rose to her feet in one graceful movement and glanced at her watch, saw that it was four. 'What time do you want to leave?'

'There's no particular hurry to get back.' He stacked the remains of their picnic in the cooler, then stored it in the boot together with the umbrella and rug.

Together they traversed the grassy slope down onto the sand and walked to the water's edge. There was a slight breeze that teased the length of her hair and gently billowed the soft material of her blouse.

The inlet was small, with a rocky outcrop bordering each point as it curved into the sea. Dominic reached for her hand, and she didn't tug it away, nor did she protest when he indicated they walk the width of the inlet.

They exchanged anecdotes, enjoyed shared laughter, and Francesca was aware of a growing friendship that was quite separate from the sexual attraction simmering between them.

The awareness was always there, sometimes just hovering beneath the surface. And on other occasions, when she became conscious of every breath she took, every beat of her heart. Part of her wanted to relax and let her emotions go any which way, and be damned to the consequences. Then logic kicked in and persuaded her to take the cautious path.

It was almost five when they returned to the car, and Dominic deactivated the alarm then unlocked the passenger door.

Francesca reached for the latch, then caught her breath as he placed an arm either side of her, caging her in an inescapable trap.

She glimpsed the darkness in his eyes in the one brief second it took for his head to descend, then his mouth was on hers, seeking what she was too afraid to give.

His lips were warm, evocative, and his tongue slid between her teeth before she had the chance to think.

He was patient, when all he wanted to do was possess. Gentle, not willing to frighten. And coaxing, persuasive, waiting for her response.

Francesca felt the betrayal of her body, the rapid pulse-beat, the slight quiver that began deep inside and invaded her limbs. The ache of awareness throbbed, radiating until she felt *alive* with sensation, and she kissed him back, luxuriating in the brush of his tongue against her own in a light mating dance that soon began to imitate the sexual act itself.

She wanted him closer, much closer, and her arms lifted to encircle his neck as she leant against him.

His arousal was a potent force, and a silent gasp

died in her throat as his hand slid down to cup her bottom, pressing her even closer.

Then he began to move, slowly, creating a barely perceptible friction that was so evocative it became almost unbearable to have the barrier of clothes between them.

A hand moved to her breast, outlined its shape, then slipped inside her blouse, beneath the lacy bra to tease the sensitised peak.

Her faint moan was all he needed, and his lips hardened as he took total possession of her mouth.

No one had kissed her with quite this degree of passion. Desire was there, raging almost out of control. His, hers. There was no sense of time or place, just total and complete absorption in each other.

It was a child's voice, pitched high and piercing, that succeeded in bringing a rapid return to sanity.

Dominic's breathing was no less heavy than her own as he buried his forehead in her hair. Her skin was warm and moist, as was his as she withdrew her arms and tried to gain leverage against the powerful body pressing far too close to her own.

'Dominic—' The protest left her lips and he lifted his head.

'I know.' With effort he straightened and unlatched the front passenger door, waited until she slid into the seat, then closed it before crossing to the driver's side.

Seconds later the engine fired and the car reversed in a semi-circle, then purred towards the gravelled apron bordering the bitumen road.

Francesca reached for her sunglasses and slid them into place, grateful for the tinted lenses. Dear heaven, they'd behaved like unrestrained teenagers! Hard after that came the thought of what might have happened had they not been interrupted.

Dominic could feel her withdrawal, and sought to prevent it. With a skilled movement he pulled onto the side of the road and brought the car to a halt.

Her face was pale, her eyes far too large as she turned towards him. 'Why are you stopping?'

He leaned an arm on the steering wheel and shifted in the seat. 'Don't close up and go silent on me.'

'What do you want me to say? Shame about the timing?' Her eyes were clear, and there was a faint tilt to her chin. 'Or perhaps I should attempt to comment about the weather, the scenery, in a banal attempt at conversation.'

'I wanted you. You wanted me. If there's any blame, it falls on both of us. Equally. That's as basic as it gets,' he said hardily.

'We were like two animals in heat. In a public area, in full sight of anyone who happened by.'

'Fully clothed,' he reminded her. 'And in control.'

Her mouth opened, then closed again. That had been *control*? What the hell was he like without it? 'Let's forget it, shall we?'

'Nice try, Francesca.' His voice was satin-smooth with a hint of dry humour as he fired the engine and eased the car back onto the road.

She wanted to hit him, and would have if the car had been stationary. He should consider himself fortunate that it took thirty minutes to reach his home at Beauty Point. By then her temper had cooled down somewhat.

As soon as the car drew to a halt she slid from the seat, closed the door, and prepared to cross to where her own car was parked.

He took his fill of her set features, the straight back, and her defensive stance. 'Running away won't achieve a thing.'

Her eyes sparked with a mixture of residual temper and pride. 'Maybe not. But right now I'm going home.'

'I intend to see you again.'

He was right, she discovered shakily. Running away wouldn't achieve anything. But she needed space, and time to *think*.

She took the few steps necessary to her car, paused, then turned back to face him. 'I have a modelling assignment scheduled for Tuesday, and a reasonable night's sleep is a prerequisite to looking good.'

He followed her to the car, and stood within touching distance. The breath caught in her throat as he took hold of her shoulders and lowered his head down to hers.

She wanted to cry out a verbal negation, but it was too late as his mouth closed over hers in a kiss that tore at the very foundation of her being.

As he meant it to do.

The knowledge frightened her on a sensual level, and made her aware of a primitive alchemy that was shattering in its intensity.

'Tuesday night. Be here, Francesca,' Dominic commanded silkily.

She was incapable of uttering so much as a word, and her fingers shook as she unlocked her car. The engine fired seconds later and she cleared the gates, aware her breathing vied in raggedness with her fast-pulsing heartbeat.

CHAPTER SEVEN

THE Leukaemia Foundation luncheon was well patronised, the venue excellent, and the fashion parade succeeded without a visible hitch.

Behind the scenes it was a different story. Annaliese arrived late and in a dangerous mood, taking pleasure in denigrating a designer, which reduced him in a very short space of time to a quivering wreck. Nothing assigned from Wardrobe pleased her, and she insisted on making changes, which caused frayed tempers, hand-wringing, and mutterings among the ranks of fellow models, not to mention everyone else involved backstage. It wasn't the worst session Francesca had participated in, but it came close.

Choosing what to wear for the evening took considerable thought, and Francesca cursed as she riffled through the contents of her wardrobe. Relaxed and casual? Or should she aim for sophistication?

The tension knotted inside her stomach as she considered crossing to the phone and cancelling out.

Her fingers momentarily stilled as Dominic's image came vividly to mind. A curse fell from her lips and her eyes clouded with pensive introspection. *What was she doing?*

Why did she have the feeling that he would appear at *her* door within an hour of her failing to appear at *his*?

After much deliberation, she selected an elegant three-piece silk trouser suit in deep emerald-green. Jewellery was minimal, and she stepped into matching stiletto-heeled pumps.

It was a glorious evening. Clear sky, blue ocean, creating a perfect background for various harbour craft taking the benefit of a slight breeze drifting over the sea.

The worst of the traffic making a daily exodus from the city was over, and Francesca experienced no delays at computer-controlled intersections.

Consequently, it was six thirty when she turned into Dominic's drive, and within minutes she cleared the gates and drew to a halt close to the main door.

She hadn't suffered such a wealth of nervous tension since her early modelling days.

Dammit, get a grip, she counselled herself silently as she pressed the doorchimes. Seconds later the door opened, and she summoned a warm smile.

'Hello.'

Dominic's eyes narrowed slightly at the huskiness evident, the faint shadows clouding her expression.

Attired in dark tailored trousers and a cream cotton shirt unbuttoned at the neck, he looked relaxed and at ease.

It would be wonderful to move into those arms and lift her face for his kiss. For a wild moment she almost considered doing just that.

'Bad day?'

Francesca offered a faintly wry smile. 'I guess you could say that.'

'Want to tell me about it?'

'What part do you want to hear?'

'Let me guess. One of the models went ballistic, a designer threw a tantrum, and whoever was in charge of Wardrobe threatened to quit.' One eyebrow slanted in humour. 'Close?'

'Close enough.'

He took hold of her arm and led her into the lounge. 'Mineral water or wine?'

'It's sacrilege, but can I have half of each?'

She felt too restless to sit, and she crossed the room to examine a small painting that had caught her attention on a previous occasion.

It was beautiful in every detail, soft blues, pinks and lilacs, a garden scene. She glimpsed the signature in the lower right corner, and almost forgot to breathe. There was little doubt as to its originality.

'You admire Monet?'

Dominic had moved silently to stand behind her, and she felt his nearness, sensed the warmth of his body.

She turned slowly to face him. 'Who doesn't?'

He handed her a tall frosted glass, and Francesca gestured a silent toast. 'Salute.'

Dinner was a casual meal of barbecued prawns with a variety of salads, eaten informally on the terrace.

'Heavenly,' Francesca accorded as she selected slices of cantaloupe and plump red strawberries from a fruit platter. There was also ice cream. Vanilla, with caramel and double chocolate chip.

She caught his teasing look, and laughed. 'You remembered.'

His eyes gleamed with latent humour. 'Will you eat it? That's the thing.'

She wrinkled her nose at him and selected a spoon. 'Just watch me!'

The view out over the harbour was magnificent as the sun began to fade towards the horizon and the shadow of dusk cast a stealthy haze. Streetlights sprang into life, regulated pin-pricks of white light spreading out over suburbia as far as the eye could see. In the distance was the heat and the beat of the city, flashing neon, bright lights, action.

Yet here it was peaceful, almost secluded, with high walls and cleverly planted shrubbery providing privacy from neighbouring properties.

'Would you like to go indoors?'

Francesca wiped her fingers on a serviette, then let her head rest back against the chair. 'I don't think I want to move.' She sighed at the thought of checking in to the airport at six the next morning.

A fashion parade at the Gold Coast Sheraton Mirage, followed by a photographic shoot, then cocktails with a public relations executive and his colleagues.

Soon she had to fly to Europe for the designer collections. After which she intended secluding herself for a week of rest and relaxation. No phones, no contact whatsoever with the outside world. Where the resort staff were bound to secrecy and the guests paid a fortune for the privilege of total anonymity.

A few weeks ago she'd been sure of her future and its direction. Now she was beginning to query what she really wanted.

'Coffee?'

Francesca turned her head slightly to look at him. 'Please.'

Dominic stood to his feet and moved indoors, and she followed, suddenly restless for something constructive to do.

In the kitchen she watched as he filled the coffeemaker, added ground beans, opened cupboards, withdrew sugar, then set out cups and saucers on the servery counter.

His hands were sure, their movements economical, and her eyes travelled, encompassing the muscular forearms exposed by the turned-back cuffs, the breadth of shoulder, the expanse of chest covered in cream chambray, up to that defined jaw, sensuous mouth, sculpted cheekbones. Those eyes, so dark, so steady as they met hers.

The breath locked in her throat at what she saw there.

Desire. Raw and primitive.

Her pulse quickened to a thudding beat that was audible to her own ears. Visible, she felt sure, as her whole body began to reverberate with answering need.

'Come here.' The command was gently spoken, and she placed her fingers onto his outstretched palm and allowed herself to be pulled into his arms.

His mouth was firm as it settled over her own,

shaping, exploring the soft contours, then nibbling at the lower fullness.

She felt his breath, warm and vaguely musky as he teased his tongue against her teeth, and she stifled a faint gasp as he began to invade the moist crevices, tasting, laving each ridge, each slight indentation, before creating a tantalising foray that deepened into total possession.

One hand slid down her spine and cupped her bottom, lifting her close up against him so that she could be in no doubt of his arousal.

She fitted as if she was meant to be there. *His.* All he had to do was convince her of that.

He could feel her acceptance of *now*, but he sensed her indecision and knew that afterwards she would feel she'd betrayed her dead husband's memory.

Francesca's hands clutched his forearms, then slipped up to his shoulders as his mouth left hers and trailed down to savour the fast-beating pulse at the base of her throat.

Her neck arched, allowing him free access, and she groaned out loud as his lips travelled down to the valley between her breasts and lingered there, caressing the soft fullness with his tongue as he edged the material down to reveal one burgeoning peak.

Dominic breathed in deeply as he tasted the wild honey that was her skin, and wanted more. Much more. He contented himself with the fact that a journey was made up of many steps. If he was to succeed, he'd have to exert patience and take one step at a time.

She wanted to feel his skin, and her fingers moved to the buttons of his shirt, freeing each one, then, not content, she pulled it free of his waistband.

Dear God, he felt good. Tight-muscled midriff, taut chest, and a generous mat of dark hair that just begged to have her fingers curl into its length.

His mouth closed over the roseate peak and he suckled shamelessly, nibbled, then caught the nipple between his teeth and took her to the edge between pleasure and pain.

Her hand slid down over the fold of his zip-fastening, trailing the rigid length before seeking the tab and slowly releasing the nylon teeth.

Fingers feathered over silk briefs to explore what lay beneath, and she felt a momentary sense of panic at the size and thickness of him.

She needed gentle persuasion, reassurance, and above all he had to show her that this was more than just sex.

'Dominic—'

His mouth took possession of her own, cutting off her protest as he utilised every ounce of skill he possessed in showing her part of his heart.

She was vaguely aware of being swept into his arms and carried up a flight of stairs to a bedroom.

His, she decided dimly as he switched on a bedside lamp on a pedestal next to a large king-size bed. Slowly he let her slide down to her feet.

Oh, God—what was she doing? 'I don't think—' She halted as he took her face between his hands and lowered his mouth to hers.

'Don't think,' Dominic bade against her lips. 'Just feel.'

I'm not sure I can give what you want. How would he react if she said those words aloud?

His teeth nipped the tip of her tongue. 'Yes.' His tongue soothed hers and his hands gentled the agitated movements of her own. 'You can.'

He wanted her so badly, *needed* the advantage of joining his body with hers so that he could show her how much he cared. How *right* this was—for both of them.

He kissed her deeply, gently coaxing in a manner that made every bone in her body turn to jelly. Dominic uttered the two words he hoped would make the difference. 'Trust me.'

Dared she? She didn't have any choice as her body proved to be its own traitorous mistress by leaning in to his kiss, giving him access to her mouth so he could plunder at will.

Her clothes, his, were quickly, easily dispensed with, and she stood almost breathless at his male beauty.

Warm, sun-kissed skin sheathed strong muscle and sinew, defining superb musculature with a sculptor's precision. Tight flanks curved down from a narrow waist, his stomach taut with an arrow of dark hair that led down to the juncture at his thighs, thickening in growth as it couched his manhood.

He stood watching her appraisal, at ease with his nudity, and her eyes skimmed the potent thickness of his arousal, skittered to his chest, and came to rest at his chin.

'Look at me.'

I just have. She lifted her face fractionally and met his intense gaze.

He reached for her, closing his hands over her arms as he slid them up to capture her shoulders.

'Open your eyes, Francesca,' Dominic bade her as his breath feathered her cheek. 'I want you to see me. Only me.'

He pulled her forward and lowered his head down towards the soft hollow at the edge of her neck.

His mouth worked an evocative magic as he savoured each and every pleasure pulse until she quivered in his arms.

Heat shimmered through every vein as she went up in flames, and he hadn't even begun.

Beautiful, he thought reverently. The faint edge of shyness appealed, even as it appalled him. She didn't possess that fierce fervour of a woman well-versed in experiencing an explosive climax. Or of one who was fully aware of the pleasure her own body could give, not only to her partner but to herself.

Slow, he determined. Slow and easy. They had the night.

Francesca groaned softly as his fingers trailed low over her stomach, then tangled in the hair curling at the apex of her thighs.

His mouth suckled at one breast, tormenting its peak into a turgid arousal, and just as she thought his touch unbearable he crossed to render a similar assault on its twin.

Fire arrowed from the centre of her being, the flame licking through her body until she felt every nerve, every cell overheating as his skilled fingers probed the moist folds, and she cried out as he

stroked the small nubbin, caressing until her whole
body shuddered and she sank against him.

A strangled gasp left her lips as he sank down
onto his knees and traced the same path with his
tongue, tasting the indentation of her navel before
savouring the line of her hipbone.

Teasing, tantalising, until he reached the soft hair
guarding entrance to her womanhood.

'Dominic—no—' The cry was one of stark dis-
belief, but he ignored the tug of her hands as she
took hold of his head.

But it was too late, much too late as she began
to experience the most intimate kiss of all. And as
his tongue wrought havoc she went up in flames,
unaware of the soft, guttural cries that emerged
from her throat, the purring pleasure as he took her
higher, or the subdued scream as he held her there
before tipping her over the edge.

Dear God, she was sweet. An intoxicating mix
of honey and musk. He suckled her moisture, savouring it like a fine wine, and held her firm when
she would have fallen.

It was too much, Francesca thought dimly as she
sought to retain a hold on her emotional sanity.
Way too much. She wanted to beg him to stop, yet
the words wouldn't formulate, let alone escape from
her throat.

His lips began a slow path over her stomach, then
travelled up to her breasts to caress each peak in
turn, settled briefly on the rapidly beating pulse at
the base of her throat, then took possession of her
mouth.

She could taste herself, then only him as he encouraged her tongue to participate in a duelling dance with his own.

It was like nothing she'd ever experienced before. Total capitulation, complete possession, and she was hardly aware of the soft mattress beneath her back until he paused to extract a small foil package from the nearest pedestal drawer.

Quick, deft movements, then his hands moulded her slight frame, caressed, then gentled as he prepared her to accept his length.

She was slick with need, aching as she'd never ached for a man, and she gasped when her flesh stung slightly as he gained entrance. She could feel the expansion of muscles and tissue, the gradual acceptance as he buried himself to the hilt inside her.

Then he began to move, slowly, almost withdrawing before carefully plunging in again, angling his shaft slightly until he felt her muscles seize and grip him. Then, when she was ready, he gradually quickened his movements until she lifted her hips to take him even deeper.

Francesca had thought it couldn't get any better, but she was wrong. His oral onslaught had heightened her senses and stimulated desire to fever-pitch. Now he took her to a higher plane, where mind, body and soul reached perfect accord and transcended anything she'd ever experienced on a sensual level.

So much for control. She had none. Nor did she want any, she decided dazedly as the spiral of sensation reached its zenith.

Perhaps she cried out as he shuddered in the

throes of his own climax, for his mouth settled over hers, soothing, gentling, as he held her close.

For a while she didn't move. Couldn't. She felt warm, and wondrously lethargic. Later she'd feel the pull of unused muscles. But for now she was content just to lie here, and savour the tumultuous aftermath of passion.

She lifted a hand and let her fingers drift down the column of his back, lingering at the indentations of his spine as she explored each vertebra until she reached the strong splay of pelvic bone.

His buttocks flexed, and she felt him swell slightly inside her.

'Uncomfortable?' His voice sounded deep and faintly husky as he grazed the hollow at her neck.

'No.' She liked the closeness, the feel of his large body, the heat and the smell of it. 'Do you want to...?' She paused, suddenly hesitant, and she felt his mouth move to form a smile.

'Disengage? Not particularly.' He shifted his weight so that he rested the bulk of it on his elbows.

He could tell from her expression, the slightly dazed look in her eyes, the soft pink tingeing her cheeks and the glow of her skin that she felt good. Lord, she excited him as few women had in the past. He wanted to take her again, to feel the tightness as she sheathed him and experience the way she moved beneath him.

Yet perhaps not so soon. There was time to tease a little, to play.

Francesca felt him shift slightly as his hands curled beneath her shoulders, then he rolled onto his back, carrying her with him.

He lifted his hands and threaded his fingers through her hair, dislodging most of the pins which held its length in what had once been an elegant French twist.

'Hmm, that's better.' His smile was slightly crooked, his eyes deep and warm as he regarded the tumble of hair falling loose about her shoulders.

He traced the outline of her mouth with his forefinger, then probed the ridge of her lower teeth.

She bit him, not hard, but sufficiently firmly to see his pupils dilate. Then she suckled the tip of his finger, swirling it with her tongue, just once, before releasing it.

So, the ball wasn't entirely in his court after all, he mused.

There was a certain degree of power in sitting astride a man. Francesca felt in control and wholly sexual, exulting in the flare of passion evident as she used her knees to exert a little leverage, then began rocking, ever so gently, watching as his eyes darkened.

There was a faint line of sweat beading his upper lip, and she leaned forward and carefully removed it with her tongue.

He let his hand slip to her breast, caressing its peak as he cupped the fullness of its twin. Beautiful and firm, the slopes were as smooth as satin to his touch.

With care he urged one engorged peak into his mouth, laving its nipple into button-hardness, and heard her almost inaudible groan as sensation pooled deep within. He could feel her response in the faint tensing of internal muscles, and his own reaction in the burgeoning of his shaft.

For what seemed hours, he had commanded her body, her senses. Now she wanted to tip the scales a little in her favour.

And she did, tentatively at first, then as her confidence grew she took complete control, riding him as hard as she dared until he grasped hold of her hips and surged into her, again and again, lifting her as he arched his body higher and higher, so that his shoulders and his feet were the only parts of him anchored to the bed.

Afterwards he cradled her close, caging her to him as he smoothed his lips across her sweat-drenched brow, his hands soothing her shuddering body until she lay limp and spent.

She must have slept, for she remembered stirring a few times and being gently rocked in strong arms before slipping back into that blissful state that was neither true sleep nor part wakefulness.

'I must go,' she murmured, not once, but twice, only to succumb to the drift of his fingers, the persuasive touch of his mouth.

'Dominic,' she groaned in the early pre-dawn hours. 'I have an early flight to catch.'

He rolled out of bed and scooped her into his arms, then carried her, protesting, into the *en suite* shower.

He bathed her, then swathed her slim form in a voluminous towel. 'Why not come back to bed?' He kissed her nose, then gently savoured that soft mouth. 'To sleep. I promise.' He brushed her lips with his own. 'I'll set the alarm and cook you breakfast.'

It was tempting, oh, so tempting. 'I really have to go home.'

He dried her carefully, offered her a selection of toiletries, then watched as she quickly donned her clothes.

What did she say to him? *Thanks, it was great*?

Dominic saved her the trouble by placing a finger over her lips. 'Take care.'

There was a sense of unreality driving through almost empty streets. There were no stars, no moon. Just an eerie pre-dawn light lifting the greyness of night.

Precisely what time was it? The illuminated clock on the dashboard revealed it was almost four. Two hours from now she needed to front up at the airport check-in counter.

Hardly enough time to snatch little more than even an hour's sleep, she decided without a trace of weariness as she garaged the car and rode the lift up to her apartment. After the night's activity, she should have been almost dead on her feet. Yet she felt strangely exhilarated, *alive* as she hadn't been in the past three years.

Inside, she brewed a cup of strong coffee and drank it black with sugar, then she checked her bags, added a few last-minute items, and made herself breakfast. Fresh juice, fruit, muesli, toast. And more strong coffee.

Awake. And waiting wasn't such a good idea, for it provided time for thought.

Last night she'd slept with a man. A hollow

laugh rose and died in her throat. Hell, *sleep* hadn't even been a consideration!

A complexity of emotions raced through her brain, clouding her perspective.

This relationship— Oh, who was she *kidding*? She groaned out loud. *What* relationship?

And what came next? Did she get to spend a night at his place, he at *hers*, escape for the occasional weekend together?

Good sex without emotional involvement. Responsible. A slightly hysterical bubble of laughter rose and died in her throat at the thought of blood tests, prophylactic protection.

Then she sobered as she became prone to introspection, and she succumbed to the inevitable feelings of guilt at having betrayed everything she held dear about Mario. The shared love, the laughter, her hopes and dreams, her fear for him. The stark replay of that fateful crash.

But tears were for the weak, and she'd shed them long ago.

With determined resolve she reset the answering machine, tidied the apartment, and at five-thirty she collected her bags, locked the door and rode the lift down to Reception, where a cab stood waiting to transport her to the airport.

CHAPTER EIGHT

THE one-hour flight to the Gold Coast was uneventful, and a friendly hostess escorted Francesca into the terminal and introduced her to a waiting chauffeur, who collected her bag and saw her seated into the rear of a luxury limousine.

There were some advantages in having acquired a degree of fame and recognition, Francesca acknowledged silently as she extracted sunglasses and slid them on.

The fact there were also many disadvantages couldn't be discounted, but this morning she was grateful for Laraine's organisational skills as the limousine headed towards Surfers Paradise.

Long, sandy beaches, gently rolling surf, deep blue ocean, and at this early morning hour a soft azure sky. The many highrise apartment buildings appeared like concrete sentinels in the distance, and as they drew close she could sense the pulse of a thriving industry dedicated to the tourist dollar.

The Sheraton Mirage was a luxury low-rise hotel, with wonderful views and access to a uniquely designed shopping complex and marina.

Unpacking was achieved in minutes, and Francesca looked longingly at the large bed, then checked her watch. She had a few hours before she needed to present herself behind the scenes in the grand ballroom downstairs. Time she could kill by browsing the shopping complex, or, what was more sensible, catching up on some lost sleep.

No contest. The bed won. And she quickly slid out of her shoes, discarded her clothes, slipped on a wrap, set the alarm, then lay down.

Not such a good idea, she decided a short while later as she dwelt on the hours she'd spent in another bed.

The only precautions taken had been Dominic's use of prophylactic protection.

Dear heaven, it had been good. Better than good. She tried to come up with a superlative, and failed. Her body still ached from his invasion, and her skin burned as she vividly recalled every detail.

He had taken his time, seducing, making everything a feast of the senses.

To become involved with a man like Dominic Andrea was dangerous, for it would be all too easy to become addicted to his brand of lovemaking, to *him*.

She'd given her heart once, and had it broken. She never wanted to feel that bereft again.

Francesca must have dozed, for she woke to the sound of the alarm and was surprised that she'd managed to sleep at all. A shower would refresh her, then she'd tend to her make-up, her hair, dress, and present herself downstairs.

There was a bowl of fresh fruit in her room, and she selected a banana, peeled and bit into it *en route* to the bathroom.

The Gold Coast Mirage was built right on the beach, with an expanse of marble floor, a stunning indoor waterfall, and a massive pool with an island bar.

The ballroom was situated on the ground floor, and one glance was all it took to determine the social glitterati had turned out in force.

The luncheon was a tremendous success, with capacity seating. Backstage chaos was minimal. There were few mishaps, and none that gained public notice.

At last she was able to escape, albeit briefly, to nibble on some finger food before the scheduled photographic shoot was due to proceed.

The photographer was over-friendly—and, worse, a toucher. Whatever image the assistant instructed Francesca to present he wanted to change—personally.

After two hours of posing in various parts of the hotel and around the pool, Francesca was almost at screaming point. He was too much in her face, and she wanted to tell him so. Almost did, on one occasion, and only barely held her tongue.

At last the final shot was taken, and she could escape to her suite for a brief respite before it was time to change and show up for the cocktail party.

Classic black, long straight skirt split to midthigh, a black sequinned singlet top, black tights, high-heeled stiletto pumps, hair piled up on top of her head with a few loose tendrils falling beside each ear, a wide gold necklace and matching bracelet. Retouched make-up.

Francesca snatched up a slim black evening purse, slipped the long gold chain over one shoulder, collected her key, and made her way to the lounge bar.

One hour, tops, then she'd retire gracefully and return to her suite, where she'd order a room service meal, then shower and fall into bed.

Several more guests began to wander into the lounge, and there were introductions, polite small talk, as well as a few informal speeches while canapés were served.

The photographer gravitated to her side and made such a nuisance of himself that when he tried to get too close she aimed her stiletto heel and brought it down on his instep.

His face whitened, then flared blood red. 'Bitch.'

Without a word she turned away from him, located the hostess, then the organiser, and exited the lounge bar.

She reached her suite, and once inside put the safety chain in position. Then she leaned wearily against the door.

Damn. She hadn't needed aggravation at the end of a long and difficult day. Following a sexually active, sleepless night.

An audible groan escaped from her lips, and she levered herself away from the door and crossed the room to the bar fridge, where she selected cold bottled water, removed the cap, and poured the contents into a glass.

Francesca kicked off her shoes, removed her earstuds, then carrying the glass into the bathroom, she began cleansing her face of make-up.

A sharp double knock on the outer door came as a surprise. She had yet to order room service, and it was way too early for the maid to turn down the bed.

She wiped her hands on the towel and crossed the room. 'Who is it?'

'Dominic.'

Dominic?

Francesca opened the door a few inches. 'What are you doing here?' The words slipped out before she could prevent them, and she saw one eyebrow lift.

'This is not the most ideal way to have a conversation,' he drawled, and she immediately freed the chain.

Attired in tailored dark trousers and an indigo cotton shirt unbuttoned at the neck, he exuded raw masculinity.

'I guess you just happened to be in the neighbourhood and decided to drop in.' As an attempt at flippancy, it failed miserably.

She didn't look as if she had weathered the day any better than he had. Fragile, definitely—and, if he wasn't mistaken, feeling acutely vulnerable.

He lowered his head and kissed her with gentle thoroughness, then pulled her into his arms and kissed her again.

When his mouth lifted fractionally from her own, she ventured, 'I should ask what you're doing here.'

He traced light kisses along her lower lip, then caught it between his teeth and bit gently. 'Should you?' His lips moved to one ear and trailed a path down her neck to one sensitive hollow, savoured it, and began exploring her throat. 'I didn't want to spend the night without you.'

Well, that certainly spelled it out. And momentarily rendered her speechless.

His soft laughter was almost her undoing. 'Did you manage to get any sleep at all?'

Francesca rolled her eyes expressively. 'I look that bad, huh?'

He lifted a hand and trailed fingers along the edge of her jaw. 'Slightly fragile.' He lowered his head and brushed his lips against her own.

'I think you can safely say that's an understatement.'

She felt rather than saw his faint smile. 'Then I think I should feed you.'

The sensual heat of his body was matched by the increasing desire in her own. If they remained in the suite they probably wouldn't get to eat at all.

'Let's walk across the road and choose one of the several restaurants overlooking the Broadwater,' she determined, and saw his lips curve with amusement.

'Safety among a crowd?'

She offered a witching grin. 'Yes.' She moved a few paces, slid her feet into heeled pumps, collected an evening bag, and tucked her hand in his.

They chose Saks, and within minutes they were seated at a window table. Soon the sky would darken and night would fall, but until it did they had a clear view of boats lining the marina and people strolling along the wooden boardwalk.

Francesca ordered a starter, a main course, and a delicious dessert.

It was an excellent meal, eaten leisurely, and afterwards they took their time over coffee. Then

Dominic settled the bill and they took the overhead footbridge to the hotel.

No sooner had they entered the main lobby than a male voice announced, 'Well, well, look who's here.'

The photographer. Slightly inebriated, and, if Francesca wasn't mistaken, out for vengeance.

He positioned his camera and reeled off some film. 'Our famed ice maiden, and escort.' His smile was vaguely feral as he subjected Dominic to a raking appraisal before focusing his gaze on her. 'No wonder you skipped the party, darling.'

With camera in hand, he held a powerful weapon. Francesca pinned a smile in place and kept walking.

'Both staying here together?'

He followed them towards the guest wing, and ventured past the 'Private—Guests Only' glass sign.

Dominic paused, then turned so that Francesca was shielded behind him. 'One step further and I'll alert the management and have charges filed against you for harassment.'

'I'm only doing my job.'

'Then I suggest you go do it some place else.'

When they reached her suite Dominic held out his hand for her key. 'Is there any need to initiate damage control?'

Francesca preceded him into the room. 'A phone call to my agent.' She tossed her evening purse down onto the nightstand and lifted the handset. 'Help yourself to a drink.'

Five minutes later she replaced the receiver and turned to find Dominic watching her.

'You've encountered this sort of problem before?'

The stalker, the pervert, the fanatic. The nightmare no one wanted.

Only her father knew about the letters she'd received for months after Mario's death. Words cut from newspapers, magazines, pasted onto blank paper and sent through the post. Compiled by a sick but shrewd mind. It had taken six months for the police to pin him down, and in that time she'd learnt to defend herself. The down and dirty kind of fighting that wasn't taught in any dojo.

Dominic caught the fleeting shadows, calculated the reason, and decided not to pursue it. There would come a time when she trusted him enough to share, and he could wait.

Francesca met his dark, discerning gaze with equanimity. 'The photographer wasn't a problem, merely a nuisance.' She crossed to a single chair and sank into it.

Last night she'd shared every intimacy imaginable with this man. Now she didn't know how to proceed. Or even if she should. A hollow laugh rose and died in her throat.

She wasn't aware of him moving. Yet his hands rested on her shoulders, soothing, gently massaging the cricks, the stiffness out of tense muscles.

It felt like heaven. 'Don't stop,' she begged, and, closing her eyes, she gave herself up to the magic of his touch.

Minutes later she groaned in protest when he

lifted her into his arms and deposited her on the
bed. With deft movements he dispensed with her
shoes, then her skirt. Next came her top.

'Dominic—'

He drew the bedcovers back, then pressed her
forward to lie on her stomach. 'Just relax and enjoy.'

Francesca thought every muscle in her body
would melt, and after the initial few seconds she
simply pillowed her head on her arms.

It was impossible to fight against the tiredness as
she reached a state of total relaxation and drifted to
sleep.

She didn't feel the mattress depress slightly as
Dominic carefully eased himself to his feet. Nor
was she aware that he pulled the covers over her,
or that he divested himself of his clothes, crossed
round to the other side of the bed and slid between
the sheets.

Francesca stirred, sensed the comfort of warm flesh
and muscle, and in the depth of her subconscious
mind she didn't question it. Merely shifted slightly
to seek closer contact. And sighed with satisfaction
as fingers lightly drifted the length of her spine.

It was a dream. A hazy, lazy vision she didn't
want to lose. The faint musky male scent mingling
with a subtle remnant of cologne merely added another dimension.

Lips grazed her cheek, then slipped to nuzzle the
hollow at the edge of her neck. Mmm, that felt
good. So good, she almost purred as the lips trailed
to her breast, savoured, then suckled gently before

sliding slowly to the curve of her waist where they traced a path to her navel, settled, succoured, and continued down over the soft concave of her belly.

Francesca moved restlessly with anticipatory pleasure, then groaned her disappointment when they began a caressing pattern close to her hip.

Fingers teased the short curls guarding her feminine core, then slid inward to stroke the sensitive clitoris.

This was one hell of an erotic dream, she mused as sensation built to a slow ache and began spiralling through her body. So acute that it seemed much too real to belong in anyone's subconscious mind.

The sweep of a hair-roughened leg against her own provided the catalyst that broke the dream and plunged her into reality.

There was a faint click, then the room flooded with light.

Francesca's lips parted, then closed, and her eyes felt incredibly large as she stared into masculine features mere inches from her own.

A dark shadow covered his jaw, a night's growth of beard that lent a raw sexuality to broad bone structure. His eyes were warm, dark, and incredibly sensual.

'Good morning,' Dominic said gently as he trailed a forefinger down the slope of her nose, then slipped down to trace the soft fullness of her mouth.

What followed was a sensual tasting—a prelude to slow and languorous loving when heightened senses flared to fever pitch, only to subside in a long sensuous aftermath.

'What time is it?'

Dominic angled his wrist in order to read the luminous dial on his watch. 'Ten past seven. Want me to order room service?'

She was hungry, and said so. At the sudden gleam in those dark eyes she quickly qualified, 'For food.'

His smile melted her bones, and he leaned forward to brush her lips with his own, then slid from the bed and stood to his feet. Unashamedly naked, his superbly muscled frame was sleek and potently male.

Far too potent, Francesca reflected as she watched him walk through to the *en suite* bathroom. Wide shoulders, a well-defined waist, tight buttocks, and long, muscular legs.

He moved with the natural ease of a physically fit man who was comfortable with his body. Assured, confident, and animalistically graceful, combining strength and power that was beautiful on an intensely male level.

As soon as the door closed behind him she pushed aside the bedclothes and reached for her robe.

Ten minutes later they walked through to the beach. White sandy foreshore and startlingly blue sea stretched as far as the eye could see to the south as the shoreline hugged the land mass.

At this hour of the morning the air held a clean freshness, warmed by the sun but without the intensity of heat that would follow as the day progressed.

'Is this going to be a brisk aerobic walk or do we stroll?' Dominic enquired as they cleared the perimeter of crunchy dry sand and gained the level, tightly packed variety fringing an outgoing tide.

Francesca cast him a considering look, taking in the casual shorts, the shirt slung carelessly across his shoulders and knotted at his chest, the peaked cap and the joggers. 'Aerobic,' she determined, and set the pace.

He shortened his stride to hers, and she shot him a winning smile.

'An attempt to expend any excess energy?'

'Mine or yours?'

His laughter was low and husky. 'Both, I imagine.' The dark, gleaming glance he threw her held more than humour, and she fought against the surge of heat flooding her veins.

He was getting too close. Much too close for her peace of mind. Invading her space, her time, and infiltrating her emotions. With a controlled determination set to destroy each and every one of her carefully erected defences.

She had a strong, instinctive feeling that with Dominic Andrea it would be all or nothing. And she wasn't anywhere near ready to examine *all*.

The beach was far from isolated. People walked, jogged, some casually, others with an intensity that spelled adherence to a fitness regime.

They reached Narrowneck, so named for the narrow strip of land separating river and ocean at that particular point, and followed the Esplanade into the heart of Surfers Paradise.

Tall, high-rise apartment buildings were positioned one after the other, and there were numerous

outdoor cafés and ice cream parlours geared to at-
tract the tourists.

'Want to stop for coffee?'

Francesca spared him a sweeping glance. 'And
croissants?' she added, feeling ravenously hungry.

He smiled as he caught her hand in his and led
her onto the boardwalk.

'A pre-breakfast snack?'

She wrinkled her nose at him and laughed. The
day seemed suddenly brighter, and it had nothing
to do with the sunshine.

They headed for the nearest café, took an outdoor
table, and Dominic ordered from the waitress.

A large table umbrella protected them from the
sun's encroaching heat, and Francesca sipped the
ruinously strong brew as she idly viewed the ocean
and the few people enjoying an early-morning
swim.

He watched as she split open a croissant and
spread each half with jam. She looked refreshed,
alert. Yet he sensed the slight defensive edge beneath her smile. If he wasn't careful, she'd attempt
to put him at arm's length.

'Want to do the return trip by sand or pavement?'
Dominic queried when they had finished.

'Sand,' she said, without hesitation, and he directed her a lazy grin.

'Not afraid I might toss you into the ocean?'

'Chance would be a fine thing.'

They walked at a measured pace, and reached the
hotel complex in good time. Francesca skirted the
large outdoor pool, sank down on her haunches to

remove her joggers, stripped down to a bikini, then slid into the cool water.

Heaven. For a few minutes she simply let her body cool, then she followed Dominic with a few leisurely laps before levering herself onto the ledge.

A towel was placed in her hand by a diligent hotel employee, and she blotted the excess moisture from her skin, aware Dominic was mirroring her actions. She stopped to collect her outer clothes, wrapped a towel round her slender curves sarong-wise, then walked ahead of Dominic to her suite.

'You take the shower first. I'll pack.'

'We'll share.'

A droll reply rose to her lips, then died. It was OK to be sassy in a public place, but here in the confines of a private suite it was a different matter. 'There's breakfast, and a plane to catch,' she managed lightly. 'With not much time to spare.'

'Five minutes of sex in the shower isn't my idea of satisfaction.' He caught her close, sliding his hands up to cup her face as he lowered his head. 'And taking a later plane isn't an option.' His mouth hovered over hers. 'So this will have to do.'

Warm, and devastatingly sensual, his mouth plundered at will, taking, giving, until she sank in against him, wanting more, much more.

When he finally broke the kiss, she was incapable of moving, and he looked down at her slightly swollen lips, the glazed, almost dazed expression in those incredibly brown eyes, and smiled.

'The shower,' he insisted gently, urging her towards the bathroom.

I've slept with him, had sex with him. What's the

big deal about sharing a shower? It isn't as if this is the first time you've shared a shower with a man.

With Mario, it had been fun and laughter.

But this was different. Way, way different.

There would be nothing humorous about sharing a shower with this man. Evocative heat pulsed through her body at the mere thought of standing a breath apart from his naked, virile frame.

She watched as he pushed down the knit boxer shorts, together with the thin black silk briefs beneath them.

Without a word she undid her bikini bra strap and discarded the scrap of Lycra, then stepped out of the matching briefs.

Water cascaded onto the tiled floor and she reached for the soap, studiously avoiding eye contact—*hell*, body contact—with Dominic.

Impossible, of course. His movements were vigorous, his use of the soap generous, and he made no attempt at modesty. Nor did his state of arousal appear to faze him.

Francesca liked to think she was adept at dealing with any situation, but this one left her fraught with nerves.

As soon as Dominic exited the shower cubicle Francesca reached for the shampoo, lathered and rinsed, then closed the water dial.

With a towel fastened round her slim form, she used the portable blowdrier on her hair, then quickly applied basic make-up and moved into the bedroom to scoop up fresh underwear and a change of clothes.

Ten minutes later she was ready, dressed in

cream tailored trousers and matching top. A long silk scarf in brilliant shades of peacock-green and blue added a dash of colour.

'We'll leave our bags with the concierge while we have breakfast.' Dominic slid the zip fastener closed on his, waiting while she added a few last minute items to hers, then caught one in each hand.

The lagoon restaurant was almost empty, consequently service was swift. Fresh orange juice, coffee, followed by cereal, fruit, toast, scrambled eggs and mushrooms.

A limousine was waiting for them, their bags stowed in the boot, as they emerged from the foyer.

Flashbulbs, one after the other in quick sequence, took them unawares.

Francesca caught sight of yesterday's fashion shoot photographer, and swore softly beneath cover of an artificial smile.

'"Francesca Angeletti and prominent Sydney entrepreneur Dominic Andrea check out of Gold Coast Sheraton Mirage Resort together. Society's hottest new couple?" Good caption, don't you think?'

So he'd done his homework. She'd suspected he might make it a mission, simply to get back at her. She didn't bother commenting, merely stepped into the rear of the limousine ahead of Dominic, glad of tinted windows and the driver's skill as he cleared the resort's entrance in record time.

With no luggage to check in, they moved directly through to the departure lounge and boarded the Boeing jet immediately prior to take-off.

'I'll pick you up at seven,' Dominic indicated as

he dropped her off outside her apartment building. At her blank look, he prompted, 'We're joining Gabbi and Benedict at the theatre, remember?'

The car slid away from the kerb before Francesca had time to say a word. Minutes later she rode the lift up to her apartment, checked her answering machine for messages, collected three faxes and sorted through her mail.

Then she walked through to her bedroom and unpacked her bag, her expression pensive as she reflected on just how she was going to deal with Dominic.

She had the strangest feeling that the ball wasn't in her court at all, and that when it came to keeping score he was way ahead of her.

The thought stayed with her throughout the afternoon, bothered her as she showered and dressed for the evening ahead, and endorsed her decision to take control of the situation.

CHAPTER NINE

FRANCESCA swept her hair into a smooth knot above her head and secured it with pins, then she completed her make-up and crossed to the walk-in wardrobe where she removed a gown in deep ruby red velvet. Its style and cut gave credit to a little known designer who, in Francesca's opinion, would soon earn kudos in the international arena. There were matching heeled pumps and an evening purse, and she added a diamond pendant and attached diamond studs to each ear.

The intercom buzzed right on time, and she reached for the receiver. 'Dominic? I'm on my way down.'

He was waiting for her in the foyer, and the sight of him took her breath away. Attired in a black evening suit, with pin-pleated white cotton shirt, he looked every inch the sophisticated social dilettante.

Yet only a fool would fail to discern the leashed power beneath the surface. Or miss the faint ruthless edge that set him apart from most men.

A valuable ally, she acknowledged silently as she slid into the front passenger seat of the gleaming Lexus. And a feared enemy.

Gabbi's husband Benedict possessed similar qualities, she reflected as Dominic eased the car off the bricked apron and onto the road. Both were hardened by the vicariousness of a cut-throat business world and the men and women who inhabited it.

Traffic into the city flowed relatively smoothly, and Gabbi and Benedict joined them at a prearranged meeting place within minutes of their arrival.

'You look fantastic,' Francesca accorded softly as she brushed her cheek to Gabbi's.

'Same goes,' Gabbi responded with a quiet chuckle.

'Shall we mix and mingle, drink in hand?' Benedict queried. 'Or would you prefer to go directly into the auditorium?'

'Dominic—*darling*. How *are* you?'

Francesca heard the breathy feminine voice and turned, interested to see who would project such an intimate greeting.

Petite and blonde, it was the same woman Dominic had been deep in conversation with at Leon's gallery a few weeks ago.

Francesca, unprepared for the arrow of jealousy, watched as the blonde clung a few seconds too long as Dominic brushed his lips to her cheek. The beautifully lacquered pink nails lingered as they trailed down his jacket, and the smile, although brilliant, didn't quite mask the edge of sadness in her eyes.

'Simone,' Dominic said gently. 'You know Gabbi and Benedict. Have you met Francesca?'

'No. Although I've often admired you on the catwalk and in the glossies.'

The lights flickered, signalling patrons to enter the auditorium and take their seats.

'Perhaps we could have a drink together some time?' Simone ventured wistfully as they parted.

Francesca noted that although Dominic's smile held warmth, he didn't commit himself to an answer, and she wondered at the sudden spurt of anger that rose to the surface and made her want to demand what Simone meant to him.

Their seats were excellent, and, although Francesca had seen a stunning cast production in London some time ago, the Australian version was excellent, and as always the music, the theme, tugged at her emotions.

When the curtain came down on the first act it was Gabbi who suggested they move into the lobby for a drink.

There was an underlying hum of excitement evident among the mingling patrons, several of whom were society matrons determined to be seen by the few photographers commissioned to cover the night.

Francesca, well-used to the careless and frequent use of the 'darling' greetings, thought if she heard just one more in the next five minutes, she'd scream.

'Damn.'

Francesca heard the softly voiced curse and looked at Gabbi, raised one eyebrow, then lowered it in full comprehension as she saw Annaliese making her way towards them through the crowded lobby.

'Want to escape to the powder room?'

'And spoil her fun?'

'You mean we get to stay and watch?'

'Oh, yes,' Gabbi said firmly, slipping her hand into Benedict's large one.

Francesca watched as Gabbi's husband cast his wife a gleaming glance and lifted her hand to his lips.

'Benedict. Wonderful to see you,' Annaliese purred as she reached them. She turned towards Dominic and cast him a smile that would have melted most men into an ignominious puddle. 'Dominic. So kind of you to take pity on Francesca.'

Grrr. Kittens played. Cats fought. 'All alone, Annaliese?' Francesca queried smoothly.

'Of course not, darling.' The smile was saccharine sweet. 'How was the Gold Coast? I believe you became embroiled with a certain photographer at the Mirage? Word has it your reaction was...' She paused for maximum effect. 'Physical.'

Francesca sharpened metaphorical claws and aimed for the kill. 'Not nearly as physical as you were in Rome, or Paris. And then there was that much publicised débâcle in Milan, if I recall?' She arched one eyebrow and offered a slight smile that was totally lacking in humour. '*Touché*, Annaliese?'

'I think we've each run the media's gauntlet at one time or another,' Benedict indicated smoothly.

It was perhaps as well the next act was due to commence. Patrons were beginning to drift back into the auditorium, and anything she might have said was lost as the music started and the lights began to dim.

The finale gained enthusiastic and well-deserved

audience applause, and at its close they rose to their feet and joined patrons exiting the auditorium.

'Let's go somewhere for supper,' Benedict suggested as they gained the car park. 'Dominic, Francesca? You'll join us, won't you?'

'Where?' Gabbi queried, and Francesca caught Benedict's faint smile as he responded.

'Double Bay.' The smile broadened. 'I doubt Annaliese will consider following us there.'

Or Simone, Francesca added silently, and admonished herself for being uncharitable.

It was almost midnight when Dominic brought the car to a halt in an allocated bay outside her apartment building.

Francesca reached for the door latch. 'Thanks for a pleasant evening.'

'We slept together last night, and made love the night before—not to mention this morning.' He caught hold of her chin and tilted it towards him. 'Tonight you want to dismiss me?'

A tiny shiver feathered through her body. 'I'm not sure I like where this is leading.'

'Define "this".'

She was afraid—of him, herself. 'You. Me.' Her eyes met his bravely. 'Soon I fly to Europe.' She felt his thumb trace her lower lip, and sensed its slight tremble at his touch. 'I won't be back in Australia for several months.'

'So...no strings?' Dominic queried in a dangerously silky voice. 'Just enjoy each other, responsibly. Alternate nights in your apartment or mine, as and when the mood takes us? Then we kiss each other goodbye and say, Hey, that was great, let's do it again some time?' He was icily angry, so much so that he wanted to shake her, *hard*. 'Is that all it meant to you?'

She could end it now, she decided dully. Say the careless words that would ensure she walked away and never saw him again.

It was what she should do—if she wanted to retain her emotional sanity.

Acute pain pierced her body and punctured her soul at the thought of never experiencing the touch of his hands, his lips grazing over her skin, or the feel of his powerful body possessing her own.

'No.'

For a few mindless seconds he didn't say anything. He was content to brush gentle fingers across one satin-smooth cheek then thread them in her hair.

'Simone threw you off balance?'

Was she that transparent? 'It's obvious she cares deeply for you.'

'We were engaged briefly in our early twenties when I was a struggling artist hell-bent on resisting my father's efforts to join him in business. Simone disliked the idea of travelling around Europe for two years on a pittance.' He shrugged. 'We argued, I walked, and Simone married someone else.'

Francesca looked at him carefully in the dim light. 'So now you're simply good friends.'

Maybe there was something in her voice, the intonation she gave, for he smiled. 'Simone is aware it can never be anything else.'

Was that supposed to be reassurance? The thought of him arousing another woman to a state of mindless abandon, his strong body urging her towards ecstasy, caused pain of a kind that made her feel ill.

'It's late.' She released the latch and opened the door. He slid out from behind the wheel and crossed round to clasp her arm. 'Dominic—'

A finger touched her lips. 'Tell me you want to be alone, and I'll go.'

She almost said yes. Then she thought how darned *good* it felt to be held in his arms, to go to sleep knowing he would be there whenever she woke through the night.

It was a tantalising vision. Part of her wanted to accept what they had together without questioning where it might lead or how it would end. Simply live for the *now*, without pondering what the future might bring.

She wanted the sweet sorcery of his touch, the sensual magic no other man had been able to evoke.

'You get to make breakfast,' Francesca capitulated lightly.

He extended a hand for her keys, and once through security they rode the lift together in silence.

Why did she feel so nervous, for heaven's sake? And alive, so gloriously wonderfully *alive*.

Such a complex mix of emotions, she acknowledged on entering the apartment.

Out of habit she slipped off her shoes, then crossed the lounge to the kitchen. 'Coffee?'

He shrugged off his jacket, folded it over a chair and followed her. 'Please. Black, one sugar.'

She took down two cups and set them on saucers.

She shouldn't feel awkward, but she did. Maybe because it was her apartment, her territory, and not the neutrality of a hotel suite.

Theatre seemed a safe topic, and they discussed other shows they'd each enjoyed, and a few dramatic productions.

Dominic replaced his empty cup, removed her own, and held out his hand. 'Turn off the lights and come admire the view with me.'

He looped his arm over her shoulders as they reached the wide expanse of floor-to-ceiling glass. A touch on the remote control module and the drapes slid back to reveal a panoramic vista. Pinpricks of electric light formed a magical pattern that extended as far as the eye could see.

Francesca made no protest when he turned her towards him, and her arms lifted, encircling his neck as his head lowered down to hers.

Mesmeric, gentle, he made kissing a sensual feast, building up a slow heat until she burned with need. Then he swept her into his arms and carried her through to the bedroom.

Her fingers were feverish as she sought to free the buttons on his shirt, and she dragged the material free from his trousers, then reached for his belt. She didn't want any barrier restricting access to his naked flesh. Or her own. And seconds later the velvet gown slid to the floor, followed by a gossamer-fine lace teddy.

They tumbled down onto the bed, and she voiced a faint protest as Dominic reached out and snapped on the bedside lamp.

'I want to see you,' he growled. 'I want you to see me.'

Francesca was past caring whether there was light or the comfort of darkness. His fingers brushed a path up her inner thigh and traced a fiery pattern before sinking into the moist tunnel in a simulation of the act itself.

Her body arched beneath him, seeking the solace he offered, then she cried out when blind need drove her over the edge.

Dominic slid into her with one powerful movement, matching each thrust to a timeless rhythm as she urged him harder and faster until they reached the pinnacle, poised there for seemingly long seconds before soaring towards a shattering climax that left them both labouring for breath.

Francesca lay limp and totally enervated, her skin moist with sweat. In her mind she'd cried out, soft, guttural sounds that had built in frequency and pitch until she was no longer conscious of where or who she was.

Dear heaven, she hadn't realised, hadn't known it was possible to lose oneself so totally in the sexual act.

To know your emotional sanity, your very existence was dependent on another caused fear of a kind she wasn't sure she wanted to deal with.

'Open your eyes,' Dominic commanded softly.

Francesca felt the drift of his fingers as they brushed her cheek, and wasn't sure she wanted to obey. For then she would have to face him, visually, physically, and acknowledge what they'd shared together.

'Tell me how you feel.'

She couldn't find the words even to begin to describe the magic euphoric state of her body and mind. Where did she start? What did she say? That her skin was a mass of acutely sensitised nerve-endings so highly attuned to *him* that it reacted to his touch as if it had received an electrical charge? Radiating heat through veins and nerve fibres to the centre of her sensual being until her entire body *sang* like a piano tuning fork?

Or perhaps she could attempt to explain the incredible meshing of mind with body? How on some deep mental level there was recognition of a kind that was like some incredible discovery, almost as if they'd known each other in another era, a former age.

The thought it could even be a possibility tore at everything she knew. It made her question *love*, and what it meant. Worse, she was forced to accept that love could assume many guises and with Mario she had experienced only one of them. And that wasn't something she wanted to examine right now.

If Dominic wanted an insight into her mind at this precise point, she would allow him to see anger. The confusion, the self-doubt. The glimmering of an enlightening revelation was hers alone.

Francesca's eyelashes fluttered upwards. 'You want assurance on how you scored?'

Something dark moved in his eyes, creating a shadow that made her feel suddenly afraid.

He had watched every fleeting expression, divined each one of them, and felt a growing frustration at being almost completely powerless to exorcise them. There was only one path to travel, that of total honesty, even if it was accorded confrontational.

'This isn't about "Was it as good for you as it was for me?" You were with me every step of the way, and we both went up in flames.'

The heat began to diminish, chilled by her own hand. A part of her bled for that loss, while another urged her towards re-establishing emotional self-preservation.

'You're a skilled lover.' Dear heaven. An understatement if ever there was one.

He was silent for a few heartstopping seconds, then he spoke in a chillingly soft voice that sent icy shivers down her spine. 'Is that all you thought it was?' His breath feathered against her cheek. *'Technique?'*

It was impossible to read his expression, and she didn't offer a word as he caught her face between both hands and tipped it so she was forced to meet his gaze.

'Francesca?' His eyes raked her features, glimpsing the defensiveness apparent in her eyes, and he swore softly beneath his breath.

'What *is* this?' Her eyes were dark and furious. 'Twenty questions?' She wanted to vent some of her anger, verbally, physically. 'What do you want to hear, Dominic? That you're the first man I've had sex with in three years?' She was like a runaway train, unable to stop. 'That having had sex with you, I'm going to allow you to be part of my life?'

He fastened his mouth on hers, effectively halting

the flow of words in a plundering possession that ravaged each and every layer guarding her soul.

It went on for what seemed an age, and when at last he lifted his head she had to struggle to regain her breath.

'I'm not giving you a choice.' His voice was deep, smoky, and filled with intent.

With an anguished cry Francesca launched herself at him, hands bunched into fists as she sought to inflict damage wherever she could connect. 'The *hell* you're not.'

She heard him grunt as she landed a blow to his ribs, and experienced a short-lived surge of satisfaction before he caught hold of one wrist, then the other and forced them behind her back.

He soon rendered her legs ineffectual by trapping them between his own, and she struggled against him, unable to gain any purchase except with her mouth, which she used without thought or aim, sinking her teeth into a hard muscled shoulder.

His retaliation was swift as he shifted slightly and took hard succour from her breast before leaving his mark on its sensitive curve.

Francesca renewed her struggle and gained nothing except a knowledge of his strength.

'Enough. You'll hurt yourself.'

She was breathing hard, her eyes molten with self-rage as she was forced to concede defeat. While he didn't look as if he was doing more than restraining a recalcitrant child.

'I hate you.' It was said almost matter-of-factly, without venom, and a muscle tensed along his jaw.

'No, you don't.'

The anger was beginning to fade a little, yet it was still there, waiting to flare given the smallest opportunity.

'Damn you.' Her eyes hurt with angry tears she refused to let fall. 'For three years I've been able to convince myself I'm doing fine.' Her vision misted. 'And I was. Until you swept into my life.' And tore it apart.

Dominic lifted a hand and traced the fullness of her lower lip with his thumb. 'I don't drive fast cars or take any unnecessary risks.'

Francesca froze with pain, then reaction set in and she reared back from him, scrambling to the edge of the bed.

'That was uncalled for, and unfair.'

'It's the truth.'

'I'd like you to leave.' Cool clear words, as cool as the ice beginning to form round her heart. She stood to her feet and snatched up a robe, then pulled it on and tied the belt.

He didn't move, and her eyes were stormy with anger as she turned to face him. 'Get dressed, and get out of here.'

Had anyone told her how beautiful she was when she was mad? With her hair tumbling onto her shoulders in disarray, her skin flushed and her eyes sparking anger, she resembled a tigress.

He slid to his feet, collected briefs and trousers and pulled them on, then stood facing her across the width of the bed.

'I'm alive,' Dominic said quietly. 'Remember that before I walk out of here.' His eyes held hers, equally as dark as her own. 'And we both lose something we could have had for the rest of our lives.'

She watched as he reached for his shirt and shrugged into it. Then he retrieved his shoes and socks and put them on.

'That's emotional blackmail.'

He paused in tying his shoelaces and cast her a long, steady look. 'It's a statement of fact.'

'A manipulative one,' Francesca corrected heatedly.

'You think I don't know how difficult it is for you to let go of the past?' There was something primitive in his expression, a ruthlessness that was harnessed, yet exigent beneath the surface. 'Or how afraid you are to let any man too close in case you get hurt?'

Her eyes were still stormy. 'It's called self-preservation. Emotional survival.'

'You think so? Destruction might be more apt.' He paused, collected his jacket and hooked it over one shoulder, aware as he said the words that he was taking the biggest gamble of his life. 'Be happy enclosed in your glass house, Francesca.'

The image was vivid, almost frightening. Inaccessible, destined always to be alone, leading an empty, shallow existence devoid of emotion. An observer, never a player. Was that what she wanted?

'Every time I take one step forward, you force me to take another,' she cried in anguish. She lifted one hand and let it fall helplessly to her side. 'I don't even know the direction, let alone the destination.'

Dominic skirted the bed and moved to stand within touching distance. 'I want it all. My ring on your finger. *Marriage*. And the right to share the rest of your life.'

Francesca felt the blood drain from her face. 'You can't mean that.'

'Can't I?' The demand was dangerously soft, and she shivered at its silent force. 'No other woman has taken control of my emotions the way you do. I doubt anyone else could.'

She was hesitant in her need to choose the right words. 'That's not a good enough reason.'

Something flared in his eyes, a flame that was quickly masked. 'What about love?'

The breath locked in her throat. *Love?* The ever-lasting kind? 'I had that once. It nearly killed me when I lost it.'

Dominic tossed his jacket onto a chair, and she was powerless to evade his fingers as he caught hold of her chin and tilted it so she had no recourse but to look at him.

'Life doesn't come with a guarantee, Francesca.' His hands slid to cup her face, his eyes dark with latent emotion. 'You make the most of what you have for as long as it's there.'

His mouth settled on her with a wild, sweet eroticism, seeking, soothing, seducing in a manner that sent the blood coursing through her veins, heating her body almost to fever-pitch.

Francesca lost all trace of time or place as she became caught up in the magic of his touch, the feel of his body as his arms shifted to bind her more closely against him.

She kissed him back, hungrily wanting as much as he could give, meeting and matching him every step of the way.

He broke free slowly, easing the pressure, the intensity, as he trailed his mouth gently over the swollen contours of her own, then he placed light, open-mouthed kisses along the edge of her jaw, traversed the column at her neck, then settled in the hollow beneath her throat.

'Will you tell me about Mario?' Dominic queried gently. 'I think I deserve to know.'

She moved back a pace, putting minimal distance between them.

Oh, God. Where did she start? Much of their lifestyle had been portrayed by media hype, some of it fact, mostly fiction. Dominic could access that any way he chose. No, it was the private story, the personal details he wanted.

'We met at a party in Rome,' she began slowly. 'We were both celebrating a personal victory. He'd won on the race circuit and I'd signed a modelling contract with a famed Italian designer.' She struggled to keep it light. 'Mario was...outgoing, gregarious.' How did you explain one man to another? Simple things, like the way he drew people, women especially, like a magnet?

'We had a whirlwind romance, and married three weeks later.' She hugged her arms tightly over her midriff in a protective gesture, and stared sightlessly ahead. 'He lived and breathed the race circuit. There was the constant adrenalin rush of the practice sessions, improving lap times, always needing to go faster, be better than anyone else. Each time he went out on the track I mentally prepared myself for the fact he mightn't come back in one piece.'

Dominic pulled her close and she wound her arms around his waist as she absorbed his strength.

They stood together like that for an age, then she felt his fingers drift up and down her spine in a soothing gesture, and there was the touch of his lips on her hair, at her temple.

'I love you.'

His hands captured her face, and she almost died at the expression in his eyes before his head descended and his mouth closed over her own.

A slight tremor shook her slim form, at what he sought to give and what she was almost afraid to take. Then she let herself go with the magic of his touch, matching his passion with such a wealth of feeling she had no recollection of anything other than the moment and the need for total fulfilment.

Their loving held a primitive quality, wild and so incredibly intense that it surpassed anything they had previously shared together. It was a long time before their breathing slowed and they lay sated, completely enervated by the depth of their emotions.

They must have slept, for Francesca stirred at the drift of fingers tracing a lazy pattern across the soft curve of her hip. Then she murmured a faint protest as the hand slipped lower and began an intimate exploration that warmed her blood and turned her body into a molten mass of malleable sensuality.

This time there was none of the heat and hunger of the night before, only a slow, leisurely loving that displayed exquisite care.

Francesca's eyes met his and held them, witnessed the strength, the purpose, and she knew she didn't want to lose him. Whatever it was they shared, she wanted the opportunity to explore it.

He saw the subtle change, felt the tension in her body begin to ebb, and sought to provide the reassurance she needed.

His mouth was gentle yet possessive as he loosened his hold and traced the indentations of her spine.

Heaven was the mutual giving and taking of pleasure, discovering, wanting to test his restraint as he tested hers until nothing else mattered but the moment. Each time they came together it seemed as if she gifted him a little bit of herself.

They slept a little, then made love whenever one or the other stirred into a dreamy state of half-sleep, part-wakefulness.

Something which happened often, Francesca acknowledged as she felt the soft passage of Dominic's lips across one cheek.

'I have an exhibition in Cairns on Saturday,' Dominic imparted close to her ear. 'Cancel any plans you have and come with me for the weekend. We'll fly up tomorrow and have a day in Port Douglas.'

From the soft dawn light filtering through the drapes, 'tomorrow' had already arrived.

She gave in to the temptation to tease him a little. 'I'll give it some consideration.'

'Minx,' he accorded huskily. 'Do you have to think about it?'

'The exhibition sounds fun. It means I get to

view some of your work. Not to mention being able to observe you in the role of artist.' She was on a roll. 'And the far north holds special childhood memories for me.'

'Is that a yes or a no?'

She smiled in the semi-darkness. 'What time do you want to leave?'

'Eight. I need to collect my bag from the house.'

She'd call her parents to let them know she'd be out of town.

His lips traced a path to the corner of her mouth. 'Hungry?'

'For you, or food?' she teased, and felt his smile. 'Both.'

She ached in places she hadn't thought it was possible to ache. 'I guess that means I don't get to snatch an hour's sleep before we need to shower, change and have breakfast?'

'Do you *want* to sleep?'

'You're offering something better?'

He didn't answer, merely showed her. It took quite a while. And afterwards he tested the speed limit, and they were last to board the flight north.

CHAPTER TEN

IT WAS hot and sultry in Cairns, with high humidity, dull skies and the threat of an imminent tropical Wet Season.

Soaring outdoor temperatures hit them like a wall of heat as they left the comfort of the air-conditioned terminal and walked the short distance to their hire car.

Francesca stripped off her cotton jacket and tossed it onto the rear seat, and Dominic loosened the top few buttons of his shirt.

The air was different up here, the pace of life less frenetic than the southern cities, and the foliage covering the ranges bordering the coastline was a lush dark green.

Port Douglas lay approximately seventy kilometres further north, with wide sweeping beaches bounding the eastern fringes and an inner harbour to the west of a narrow promontory.

Sugar cane country, Francesca mused as they passed acres of freshly farrowed paddocks. Mechanical planting and cutting now. Only firing the cane remained the same as it had in years gone by. Small rail tracks crossed the road at intervals, connecting one farm to another, so that cut cane could be loaded and transported to the mill.

She remembered holidaying in this region as a child, visiting Italian grandparents who'd owned vast cane holdings and a farmhouse that was filled with exotic cooking smells, much love and laughter. Now her grandparents lay buried side by side, and the land had been divided and sold off in part to developers.

There were several resorts bordering each side of the four-kilometre stretch leading into Port Douglas, and Dominic took the long, curved driveway that led to the exclusive Sheraton Mirage.

Their suite was luxurious, with sweeping views of the ocean. 'I need to make a couple of calls,' Dominic relayed as he stowed their bags. 'Then we can swim, explore, drive up onto the Tableland. Or,' he suggested, closing the space between them, 'stay here and order in as the mood takes us.'

Francesca moved into his arms and lifted her face for his kiss, loving the feel of his mouth on hers, the gentle possession that rapidly led to hunger of a kind neither of them wanted to deny.

He was a caring lover, pacing his needs to her own, then, when he'd driven her to the point of wildness, he tipped her over the edge and held her as she fell.

There was no sense of time or place in the long afterplay. The drift of fingers, the exploration by lips and the slow sensual tasting that teased and lingered, incited, until only total fulfilment would suffice.

It was dark when they rose from the bed, showered and dressed.

Dominic regarded her quizzically as she applied minimum make-up and stepped into heeled sandals.

'Does this mean you'd prefer to eat dinner in the dining room?'

Francesca's eyes held a devilish gleam, and her smile was almost wicked. 'I need food as an energy boost to last me through the night.' She touched her lips with the tips of her fingers and blew him a kiss. 'Besides, it would be nice to enjoy the ambience, don't you think?' The corners of her mouth lifted with delicious humour. 'A light white wine, seafood. The local barramundi is superb, and when we've had coffee we can stroll through the grounds.'

Dominic pulled on trousers, added a polo shirt, and slid his feet into loafers. 'Just remember this was your idea.'

A soft bubble of laughter emerged from her throat. 'Think of the anticipation element.'

He bestowed upon her a brief, hard kiss, then caught hold of her hand. 'I'll bear that in mind.'

The dining room was well patronised, the food excellent and the wine superb. They lingered over coffee, then elected to traverse the extensive pool perimeter before retreating to the covered walkways linking the resort's various guest villas together.

Dominic's arm curved round her shoulders, pulling her close, and she smiled in the semi-darkness. It felt good. Better than good. It felt *right*.

Their air-conditioned suite was blessedly cool after the heat of the night, and it was she who moved into his arms, pulling him close for a long, hungry kiss.

Clothes soon became an impossible barrier, and

they took pleasure in the process of discarding them before tumbling down onto the bed.

This time there was no feeling of guilt, no sense of shame. It was Dominic's features she saw, the passion she experienced solely for him.

In the morning they woke late, enjoyed a leisurely breakfast, then checked out of the resort and took the inland highway through Julatten and Mount Molloy to Mareeba, before heading east via the Kuranda range to Cairns.

A late lunch, a check of the gallery, then they returned to their hotel for dinner. Invited guests were scheduled to arrive at the gallery at eight, and a limousine was to be despatched to the hotel to transport them the two blocks distant.

Francesca had selected black Armani evening trousers and matching jacket, high-heeled pumps and discreet gold jewellery. Her make-up was understated, with emphasis on her eyes.

'Sensational,' Dominic commended with a slow sweeping appraisal that made her heart beat faster. He fixed his black bow tie, adjusted cufflinks, then shrugged into his suit jacket. The look was that of a high-powered business executive, sophisticated, at ease and in total control.

Dominic reached into his pocket and withdrew a slim jeweller's case. Inside was an exquisite gold chain, and she watched as he extracted it and fastened it around her neck.

His eyes met hers and held them as he lifted her left hand and pressed the intricate gold band to his lips.

The gesture shocked her, and a sensation akin to

pain settled deep in her heart. She could only look at him in silence, incapable of uttering so much as a word, and she made no protest as he caught hold of her hand and led her from the suite.

The gallery was in a converted old Queenslander-style home, with wide covered verandahs bordering each of the four external walls. Double French doors led onto the verandah from every room, and the effect was one of rambling spaciousness.

Dominic was greeted effusively, Francesca recognised, and accorded equal reverence.

There was little opportunity to wander at will and admire the exhibited paintings before the first of the guests began to arrive.

'You're a hit,' Francesca murmured later as the gallery filled and the erudite examined and essayed an opinion as they conferred with apparent knowledge on style and form. A 'Sold' sticker appeared on one painting after another.

'Me, or my art?' Dominic teased, and saw her eyes gleam with hidden laughter.

'Both,' she said succinctly. 'Think you can hold things together for a while?' There was no doubt he could. 'I intend to appraise the exhibits.'

'Why is it that your opinion makes me nervous?'

She cast him a musing smile, then saw that he meant it. 'Afraid I might get a glimpse of your soul, Dominic?'

'Perhaps.'

How did one judge the complexities of a man who was capable of such artistic expression? Was any part of it an extension of the man himself, or merely a practised style?

'He's very talented, don't you think?'

Francesca turned at the sound of a male voice, and smiled at the elderly silver-haired gentleman. 'Yes. Yes, he is.'

He indicated the abstract. 'What do you see in this?'

'It intrigues me,' she said honestly. 'I look for hidden meanings, and find none.'

'Precisely. But one cannot easily give up the search for a key which could unlock the puzzle, hmm?'

'You're right,' she conceded slowly, and he lifted an imperious hand.

'I shall buy it. As an investment it will increase threefold in value over the next few years. It will also provide my guests with a conversation piece.' He lowered his hand as an assistant hurried forward. 'Now, my dear, what takes your eye?'

He accompanied her from one room to another, his interest keen, his charm and wit entertaining. It was more than an hour before Francesca rejoined Dominic, and she met his faintly raised eyebrow with a smile.

'I've been conversing with a very interesting gentleman.'

'Samuel Maxwell, art critic and collector,' Dominic acknowledged.

'He thinks you're very talented.'

His eyes gleamed with mocking humour. 'I'm honoured.'

'He bought an abstract.'

'And flattered,' he said steadily. 'Maxwell is selective.'

'There you go,' she said lightly. 'Another fan.'

'And you, Francesca. Are you a fan?'

'Of the art, or the man?'

She was saved from answering when his attention was caught by a dowager of generous proportion who flirted outrageously. Francesca cast him a faintly wicked smile, and moved to the far side of the room.

It was a further hour before they could slip away. The evening was, according to the ecstatically fulsome gallery owner, a tremendous success.

A limousine returned them to their hotel, and they took the lift to their floor.

'Tired?' Dominic queried as they entered their suite.

'A little.' She slipped off her shoes and loosened her jacket.

He lifted a hand and lightly traced the gold chain to where it nestled in the valley between her breasts. 'You have beautiful skin.'

Her eyes lightened with humour. 'Are you seducing me?'

'Am I succeeding?'

Every time. She had only to look at him and her body went into sensual overdrive. All evening she'd been supremely conscious of him, part of the scene yet apart from it. And knew that he was equally as aware of her as she was of him. It had been evident in every glance, the touch of his hand whenever she drifted into his orbit, the warmth of his smile.

He made her feel so incredibly alive. A warm, sensual woman in tune with her own sexuality and aware of its power.

It was an awakening, a knowledge that heightened the senses and brought another dimension to the physical expression of shared sex. The body and mind in perfect accord with that of another. Mutual pleasuring gifted freely without self-thought.

Francesca lifted her arms and pulled his head down to hers, loving the feel of his lips as they grazed across her cheekbone, traversed her jaw, then settled with unerring accuracy on her mouth.

They had the night. Tomorrow they'd board a flight south and resume the hectic tenure of their individual lives. But for now it was enough to savour the loving.

Francesca awoke slowly to the light trail of fingers creating a pattern over the concave of her stomach, and she felt the rekindling of desire as lips settled fleetingly on one shoulder and trailed a path to her breast.

She could feel the faint rasp of his night's beard as it grazed lightly over her skin, and she gave a soft, exultant laugh as he caught her close and rolled onto his back.

There was a feeling of power in taking control, and he allowed her free rein as she tantalised and teased, then it was he who set the pace and she who clung to him in a ride that tossed her high, so high she had no recollection of anything except acute sensual pleasure, and the knowledge he shared it with her.

Long afterwards she lay cradled against his chest, his arms caging her close as he smoothed her tumbled hair and stroked fingers over her silken skin.

It was late when she woke, and they showered

together, ordered in breakfast, then dressed and checked out in time to connect with the Sydney flight.

Several hours later they disembarked, exited the airport terminal, and entered into the stream of traffic heading towards the city.

'I have to be in Melbourne tomorrow,' Dominic informed her as he negotiated a busy intersection, and Francesca felt a sense of loss.

'When will you be back?'

'Wednesday at the earliest. Probably Thursday.'

She'd miss him. 'I have a photographic session Wednesday, another scheduled for Thursday.'

They were traversing the Harbour Bridge before she realised he hadn't taken the Double Bay turnoff.

'Dominic—'

'Stay with me tonight.'

She didn't need to think, didn't *want* to think. She'd have enough time to do that while he was away.

It was after eight the next morning when Dominic deposited Francesca outside her apartment building on his way to the airport.

She rang Rick, then Sophy, caught up with Gabbi, and had a long conversation with her agent. An international fax from her mother-in-law's Italian solicitor needed an immediate response, which entailed a search through copies of legal correspondence.

Lunch comprised a salad sandwich followed by fruit, and she cooked pasta for dinner.

Dominic called her at nine, and the sound of his voice produced an unbearable longing. 'Missing me already?'

You don't know how much. 'A little.'

'It'll keep, Francesca.'

She hadn't fooled him in the slightest. 'Sleep well,' she lightly mocked, and she heard his soft chuckle.

'Promises?'

'Maybe.'

It was late when she slipped into bed, and she lay awake for an age, damning her inability to fall asleep. After an hour she switched on the television and changed channels for a while. Her head felt heavy with tiredness, and she lifted the weight of hair from her nape in an effort to ease the kinks.

Her fingers touched on the gold chain at her neck, and she absently traced its length as she thought of the man who had put it there, and why.

What she'd had with Mario had been special. No one could take it away. But would he have wanted her to live the rest of her life alone? To deny herself happiness and love—a different kind of love perhaps—and children, with another man? Somehow she didn't think so.

Without questioning her actions she drew off Mario's wedding ring and attached it to the chain, feeling the weight nestle in the valley between her breasts.

There were roses waiting for her in Reception when she entered her apartment building late the following afternoon, and she rang Dominic on his cellphone, only to discover he was in a meeting and unable to talk freely.

'I can say anything, and you'll be hampered in your response?' Francesca teased.

'I can always reschedule.'

She laughed. 'For something terribly decadent, with fresh strawberries and expensive champagne?'

'Is that a definite?'

'Would you prefer yoghurt or whipped cream?'

'Count me in.'

'I'm offering seconds.'

'That, too.'

'What would your associates think if they knew you were indulging in mild phone sex?'

His voice deepened. 'I'll look forward to settling with you in a day or two.'

She gave an irrepressible chuckle. 'I'll hold that thought.'

It was no easier to summon sleep than it had been the night before, and Francesca lay awake in the darkness caught up in a web of reflective thought.

Love. Was *this* what it was? An inability to *think*, to function without him? To want, *need* with such intensity it became difficult to focus on anything else?

Wednesday's fashion shoot went way over time, and an unexpected summer shower saw Tony transfer the shoot indoors, to his studio, before moving on as scheduled to a major city department store.

It was almost closing time when the final shot was taken. Staff were packing up, and only a few last-minute shoppers remained.

In the changing room Francesca stepped into cotton trousers, fastened the zip, then pulled a skinny-rib top over her head.

The store's background piped music clicked off as she stepped into heeled sandals and gathered up her bag.

'Who the hell are you, and what are you doing here?'

'Waiting for Francesca,' a deep male voice drawled in response.

Dominic.

She smoothed nervous fingers over the length of her hair, then emerged from the changing room to see Tony regarding Dominic with hard-eyed suspicion.

He turned towards Francesca as she moved forward. 'You know this man?'

Her eyes met Dominic's, and what she saw there made her catch her breath. Then she smiled. 'Yes.' She didn't hesitate, just walked straight into his arms and raised her face for his kiss.

Dominic was very thorough, and it was several minutes before he lifted his head. 'The lady is with me,' he said with deadly softness, for the benefit of anyone who might have held the slightest doubt. Then he looked down at her. 'Isn't that so?'

He was asking much more than that, and she gave him his answer. 'Yes.'

Later, much later, they lay entwined in the shadowy dark hours of night, sated and deliciously drowsy after a long loving.

'You are going to marry me?'

Francesca lifted a hand and gently traced a finger over the length of his jaw. 'Am I?'

Dominic let his teeth nip at a delicate swell of flesh, felt her shudder, and sought to soothe the tiny bruise with a gentle open-mouthed kiss.

'That was meant to be a statement, not a question.'

'Ah.' She smiled in the darkness. 'Being masterful, are we?'

'Soon.' The insistent undertone made her want to tease him a little.

'Next year?' The query earned her an evocative kiss that made her forget everything.

'Next week.'

'That could be difficult.'

She felt rather than heard his soft laughter as he trailed his mouth down the edge of her neck. 'Nothing is difficult.'

No, it wasn't, if you had the money to pay a horde of people to organise everything.

'Like to hear what I have in mind?'

She let her fingers traverse the indentations of his back, then conducted a slow sweep to one hip. 'Why is it I get the feeling you've already set a plan in motion?'

'A ceremony in the gardens at my home, a celebrant, family and immediate friends.'

It sounded remarkably simple. And romantic. Francesca could almost see it. A red carpet rolled out on the spacious lawn, glorious stands of trailing roses framing the gazebo. She even had a dress she'd never worn that would be perfect.

She sensed the faint tightening of muscles beneath her straying fingers, felt the increased beat of his heart and was unable to continue teasing him. 'OK.'

'OK? That's it?'

'Yes,' she said gently. 'There's just one consideration.'

'Tell me.'

'I'm due in Milan, remember? Then Paris.'

'My darling Francesca,' Dominic declared with deceptive indolence, 'I'll not only be sharing your flight—' he placed his lips against a particularly vulnerable part of her anatomy and felt her indrawn breath '—I'll be standing at the rear of every function room wherever you appear on the catwalk.' He suckled gently and felt her fingers rake through his hair. 'And occupying your bed every night.'

'Mmm,' she murmured with satisfaction. 'I was hoping for that.'

His laugh was low and smoky. 'Should I be brave and ask which has priority?'

As if he needed to ask! Her lips curved to form a winsome smile. 'It's nice to share travel with a companion.'

'Really?'

'Uh-huh. And of course it will be reassuring to know you're in the audience.' The smile widened. 'Although you should be warned that designers are temperamental creatures who won't tolerate distractions.'

'Guess I don't get to go backstage.'

'Not if you value your life.'

'They're likely to get physical?' He was deliberately baiting her, and she responded in kind.

'No, but I might.' Too many women in various stages of undress wasn't something she felt inclined to share with him.

'You've left out something.'

'I have?' She gave a tiny yelp as he rolled onto his back and carried her with him. A slow, sweet smile lightened her features and she lifted her arms high in a graceful cat-like stretch. 'Oh, yes. You get to share my hotel suite each night.'

'Witch,' Dominic accorded lazily.

It was a while before Francesca could summon sufficient energy to talk.

'A rooftop apartment in Paris, and a delayed honeymoon would be a nice way to bring my career to a close.'

Something jerked at his insides, and he carefully controlled it. 'You're thinking of giving up modelling?'

She hadn't needed to give it much thought. 'Professionally.'

There was silence for a few seemingly long seconds. 'Don't you want to ask me why?' Francesca queried gently.

This was one time he found it difficult to coordinate the right words. 'Tell me.'

'I want to have your child. Children,' she corrected. 'That is, if you—'

Dominic didn't allow her to finish as he brought her head down to his, and his mouth was an evocative instrument as he kissed her with such passionate intensity it melted her bones.

When at last he lifted his head, she could only press her cheek into the curve of his neck, and a slight tremor shook her slender frame as he cupped her face and shifted it so that he could see her expression in the slim stream of moonlight arcing across the room.

'You'll make a beautiful mother,' he said gently.

She felt the prick of tears, and consciously banked them down, but not before he'd glimpsed the faint diamond-glitter drops on the edge of her lashes.

His mouth possessed hers with a soft, evocative hunger that was so incredibly tender she could almost feel her whole body sigh in silent acceptance of a joy so tumultuous it transcended any rationale.

CHAPTER ELEVEN

THE limousine carrying Francesca, Gabbi and Katherine swept smoothly across the Harbour Bridge, then headed towards Beauty Point.

It was a glorious summer afternoon, the sky a clear azure with only a nebulous drift of cloud to mar its perfection.

Francesca lifted a hand and absently fingered the single strand of pearls at her neck. It held a pendant, a pearl teardrop surrounded by diamonds. There were earstuds to match. Dominic's gift to his prospective bride.

Her gift to him was simplistic, but meaningful. A secret smile curved her lips, and her eyes softened as she imagined his reaction.

Her fingers sought the slim gold chain, and failed to find it. A slight frown creased her forehead. It must be directly beneath the pearls. She remembered taking it off before she showered...and had a mental image of lifting the pearls from their flat jeweller's box.

She'd left the chain on the bedside pedestal.

'We have to go back.' The words slipped out before she was even aware she'd voiced them.

'But we're almost there,' Gabbi protested. And at the same time Katherine expressed in consternation, 'Francesca, we'll be late.'

174

Somehow she didn't think Dominic would mind. Although first she needed to instruct the driver, then she had to make a call from the car phone. When both were achieved, she sank back against the cushioned seat.

'Are you going to tell us what this is all about?' Gabbi asked curiously.

'I left Dominic's gift at my apartment.'

'You could have given it to him later,' Gabbi rationalised.

'Yes,' Francesca agreed, 'I could. Except it wouldn't be the same.'

Thirty minutes later the limousine drew to a halt at the apex of Dominic's driveway, and Francesca slid out from the rear seat to stand still as Gabbi and Katherine ran a last-minute check on the exquisitely pale champagne gold sheath dress with its cream antique lace overlay Francesca had chosen to wear for her wedding.

Gabbi grinned and gave her approval. 'Let's get this show on the road.'

Rick was waiting inside the house, and he came forward the instant they entered the lobby.

'Francesca.' He caught hold of her shoulders and held her at arm's length. 'Everything OK?'

'Very much OK,' she assured gently as she leaned forward and brushed his cheek with her own. She made an attempt to lighten the situation. 'That is, if Dominic is still waiting out there for me.'

'With considerably more patience than most men would be able to summon in similar circumstances,' Rick accorded drily.

'Then let's not keep him waiting any longer, shall we?' Francesca suggested lightly.

The gardens were beautiful, the flowers and shrubs clipped to perfection, and the lawn a carpet of green.

There were a few guests seated behind members of her immediate family, but she hardly saw them. Her focus was centred on the white-painted gazebo and the tall, dark-suited figure who stood watching her progress as she walked the length of red carpet with Rick at her side.

Francesca looked into Dominic's eyes and saw everything she needed to know laid bare. Her own eyes misted, and there was a slight quiver to her lips as she summoned a slow, sweet smile.

A few more steps and she'd be able to place her hand in his, feel its warm strength and accept what he offered for the rest of her life. There was no lingering doubt or apprehension, only love.

Dominic gathered her in close and kissed her with such passion it was all she could do to keep a hold on her sanity.

It could have lasted seconds or minutes, she had no recollection of the passage of time.

Minutes, she decided, as she heard the sound of faint amusement from those assembled behind her.

'Mr Andrea, it's usual to kiss the bride *after* the ceremony.'

'Believe me, I intend to do it then, too,' Dominic drawled with musing indolence.

The celebrant chuckled, then cleared his throat. 'Shall we begin?'

'Could you wait just a moment?' Francesca requested. 'There's something I need to do first.'

She turned towards Dominic, caught his faintly
raised eyebrow, and smiled as she lifted both hands
to her neck. Seconds later she placed the long thin
gold chain holding Mario's wedding ring in the
palm of his hand.

Would he realise the significance of her action?
Know that by gifting him Mario's ring she was willingly giving Dominic her heart? All of it.

Francesca wasn't aware she was holding her
breath until his mouth curved into a warm smile,
his eyes liquid with comprehension, and she released it shakily, only to catch it again as he lifted
her left hand to his lips and kissed the bare finger
awaiting the placement of *his* wedding band.

'Thank you,' he said gently.

'I thought it would mean more to you than anything else I could gift you,' she responded softly,
adding with a faintly wicked smile, 'At this moment.'

His eyes flared, then became incredibly dark.

Francesca turned a radiant face towards the celebrant. 'We're ready.'

It was a simple ceremony, and afterwards
Dominic kissed his wife with such incredible gen-
tleness the men among the guests shifted uncom-
fortably and the women were seen to blink rather
rapidly.

The food was superb, with catering staff serving
at tables set out on the wide terrace with its pano-

ramic view of the harbour. The cake was cut and photographs were taken.

Francesca barely remembered tasting a morsel, and she merely sipped from a flute of champagne.

She was supremely conscious of Dominic seated at her side, the touch of his hand, the way his body brushed against her own. His eyes, those dark, almost black depths, liquid with emotion whenever she caught his gaze, tugged at an answering need deep inside her.

A musing smile curved her lips as he leaned his head close to her own.

'I guess it wouldn't do to leave early.'

She turned her head slightly and brushed her lips against his. 'I don't think so.'

'Damn,' he cursed lightly.

Her lashes curled upwards, revealing a wicked gleam in those stunning liquid brown eyes. 'Another hour won't kill you.'

His mouth curved in answering humour. 'It might.' His lips feathered close to her ear. 'I have this pressing need to...' In a voice as soft as the finest silk he proceeded to explain what he meant to do the instant they were alone.

Her body began to melt, curving into his like warm wax. 'I think we should mingle,' she said unsteadily. 'Otherwise we're in danger of shocking the guests.'

His mouth drifted over hers, savoured briefly, then he caught hold of her hand.

Together they circled the tables, lingering, laughing, until it was time to change, collect their bags

and slip into the limousine that would transport
them to a city centre hotel.

'This is…' Francesca paused in the centre of a
sumptuous penthouse suite. 'Overwhelming.'

Dominic closed the door, then walked to where
she stood. '*You* overwhelm me.' He lifted a hand
and brushed his fingers against her cheek. He didn't
care that they were slightly unsteady as he glimpsed
the emotion evident in her wonderfully luminous
eyes. For him. Only him.

'I love you,' he said gently. 'Today. All the to-
morrows.' He traced the curve of her mouth with
his thumb, felt its soft fullness, and wanted the
sweetness inside. 'I can promise never to willingly
hurt you. You have my heart, my soul.'

She ached so much, so deeply, that her eyes hurt
with the strength of her emotions. 'I didn't think
love could happen twice.' She had to blink to keep
the prickle of threatening tears at bay.

He smiled and drew her close, his breath catching
as her arms lifted to his shoulders then crept to
encircle his neck.

Her lips touched his, opening like the petals of a
rose as he took possession, deepening the kiss until
she lost recognition of everything except the man.

He filled her senses and made her *want* as he
offered the promise of heaven on earth. More. He
delivered. And then some.

But then, so did she. Willingly, wantonly. Gifting
him more than her body. Everything.

Tonight there was none of the urgency, little of
a driven need. Just a long, slow loving that took

them to the heights several times and beyond. They slept a little, then woke to exult in each other again until the sunlight chased away the shadows of night.

Francesca lifted a hand, pushed back her tangled hair, then she met his eyes and smiled. 'I love you.'

Her pulse-beat had returned to normal after a passion so incredibly tumultuous every nerve-end still hummed with acute sensation.

'Do you know how much it means to me to have you say that?' Dominic queried huskily.

His hand began to drift as his fingers traced a lazy pattern across her stomach, explored her navel, then moved to tease the whorls of hair at the apex between her thighs.

The scent of her drove him crazy. Her skin was so delicate, so fragile, he almost felt afraid to touch her. Yet she shared his hunger, and exulted in his possession, until he forgot who he was in the need to gift her not only his body but his mind. It was frightening to give up so much power, to lay oneself so open and bare. Yet he doubted she would ever use the advantage against him.

His head lowered to her breast and he began grazing a tender nipple with the edge of his teeth.

The tug of renewed desire arrowed through her body, and she trailed her fingers across his back, exploring the muscular ridges, aware of the strength and the power, and wondered for the nth time how she had existed, believed she'd lived, before meeting this man who was now her husband.

Almost as if he read her mind his head lifted and he settled his mouth over hers, soothing, gentling, marking her as his own as surely as if he'd branded her flesh with fire.

The strident peal of the telephone sounded loud in the silence of the room, and Dominic shifted, then reached for the receiver.

'Our wake-up call?' Francesca hazarded as Dominic replaced the handset.

'We have fifteen minutes to shower and dress before room service deliver our breakfast.'

She looked at him with mock solemnity. 'It was your idea to book an early-morning flight to Athens.'

His eyes held a wicked gleam. 'Ah, but I had the foresight to organise a stop-over *en route*.'

A smile tugged the edge of her mouth. 'How thoughtful.' The temptation to tease him a little was irresistible. 'Shall we hit the shower separately or together?'

'You really want me to answer that?'

She slid out from the bed and walked unself-consciously towards the adjoining bathroom. When she reached the door she turned and shot him a tantalising smile. 'Can't stand the heat, huh?'

She'd barely made it to the shower cubicle when firm hands fastened around her waist, lifting, turning her until she was positioned astride his hips.

A laugh bubbled up in her throat, then died as he bestowed upon her a brief, hard kiss before lowering his mouth to settle at the acutely sensitive pulse at the base of her throat.

She shuddered as sensation spiralled through her body, and she arched up against him, groaning out loud as his teeth closed over one swollen nipple, teasing, suckling, until she was almost driven to the brink of sanity.

Francesca cried out when he shifted his head and rendered a similar salutation to the twin peak.

His eyes were impossibly dark when they finally met hers, and she felt herself drowning in those dark depths, seriously adrift as his mouth lowered to possess hers in a kiss that echoed the deep, pulsing thrust of his powerful body.

She rose with him, wrapping her arms round his neck as she held on and gloried in their shared passion.

And afterwards she buried her lips in the hollow of his neck, too enervated to move as her racing heart slowed and steadied to its normal beat.

His hand travelled slowly up and down her spine, soothing as he pressed his lips to her hair.

It was heaven to rest against him like this, to feel that what they shared meshed the physical and spiritual in a rare coupling that few were fortunate to attain.

She felt him burgeon inside her, sensed the increased urgency, and rode with him one more time, slowly, gently, as if they had all the time in the world.

A hard double knock on the outer door brought them both back to the reality of the day, and a faint curse escaped Dominic's lips as he carefully lifted her down onto her feet.

'Breakfast.' He reached for a towelling robe and tugged it on, then he leaned forward and pressed a gentle kiss to her faintly swollen mouth. 'Stay there. I'll be back in a minute.'

She could imagine him crossing the suite, opening the door, signalling for the waiter to deposit the tray.

The thought of cereal and fruit, scrambled eggs and toast gave her an appetite, and she reached for the dial, set it to warm and released the lever.

Seconds later the glass door slid open and Dominic stepped into the stall, removing the soap from her fingers as he lathered every inch of her skin. Then he held out the soap. 'Your turn.'

'Oh, no,' Francesca denied, laughing softly. 'You're on your own.' She reached up and pulled down his head for one brief, soft kiss. 'Too many challenges and we'll not only miss breakfast, we'll miss the plane.' She shot him a dazzling smile. 'Besides, I'm *food* hungry.'

He let her go, with a devilish smile that hinted her escape was only temporary.

As the giant jet taxied down the runway Dominic reached for her hand and lifted it to his lips.

'No regrets?'

Francesca looked at those strong features, the raw emotion evident in his eyes. She lifted shaky fingers to his cheek, then trailed them to the edge of his mouth, and stifled a gasp as he drew the tips in between his teeth. 'Not one.'

He reached for her, uncaring of the fellow passengers sharing the first-class cabin, or the hostess who was waiting to serve them.

His mouth on hers was incredibly gentle, and when he lifted his head he glimpsed the faint shimmer of tears.

'We have a lifetime.'

Her bones liquefied at the warmth evident in those dark eyes. 'Yes,' she affirmed simply.

Carpe diem. Seize the day. And she would, with both hands, and rejoice in every one of them.

Head Down Under for twelve tales of heated romance in beautiful and untamed Australia!

Here's a sneak preview of the first novel in THE AUSTRALIANS

Outback Heat **by Emma Darcy**
available July 1998

'HAVE I DONE something wrong?' Angie persisted, wishing Taylor would emit a sense of camaraderie instead of holding an impenetrable reserve.

'Not at all,' he assured her. 'I would say a lot of things right. You seem to be fitting into our little Outback community very well. I've heard only good things about you.'

'They're nice people,' she said sincerely. Only the Maguire family kept her shut out of their hearts.

'Yes,' he agreed. 'Though I appreciate it's taken considerable effort from you. It is a world away from what you're used to.'

The control Angie had been exerting over her feelings snapped. He wasn't as blatant as his aunt in his prejudice against her but she'd felt it coming through every word he'd spoken and she didn't deserve any of it.

'Don't judge me by your wife!'

His jaw jerked. A flicker of some dark emotion destroyed the steady power of his probing gaze.

'No two people are the same. If you don't know that, you're a man of very limited vision. So I come from the city as your wife did! That doesn't stop me from being an individual in my own right.'

She straightened up, proudly defiant, furiously angry with the situation. 'I'm *me*. Angie Cordell. And it's time you took the blinkers off your eyes, Taylor Maguire.'

Then she whirled away from him, too agitated by the explosive expulsion of her emotion to keep facing him.

The storm outside hadn't yet eased. There was nowhere to go. She stopped at the window, staring blindly at the torrential rain. The thundering on the roof was almost deafening but it wasn't as loud as the silence behind her.

'You want me to go, don't you? You've given me a month's respite and now you want me to leave and channel my energies somewhere else.'

'I didn't say that, Angie.'

'You were working your way around it.' Bitterness at his tactics spewed the suspicion. 'Do you have your first choice of governess waiting in the wings?'

'No. I said I'd give you a chance.'

'Have you?' She swung around to face him. 'Have you really, Taylor?'

He hadn't moved. He didn't move now except to make a gesture of appeasement. 'Angie, I was merely trying to ascertain how you felt.'

'Then let me tell you your cynicism was shining through every word.'

He frowned, shook his head. 'I didn't mean to hurt you.' The blue eyes fastened on hers with devastating sincerity. 'I truly did not come in here to take you down or suggest you leave.'

Her heart jiggled painfully. He might be speaking the truth but the judgements were still there, the judgements that ruled his attitude towards her, that kept her shut out of his life, denied any real sharing with him, denied his confidence and trust. She didn't know why it meant so much to her but it did. It did. And the need to fight for justice from him was as much a raging torrent inside her as the rain outside.

MEN at WORK

All work and no play? Not these men!

April 1998

KNIGHT SPARKS by Mary Lynn Baxter

Sexy lawman Rance Knight made a career of arresting the bad guys. Somehow, though, he thought policewoman Carly Mitchum was framed. Once they'd uncovered the truth, could Rance let Carly go...or would he make a citizen's arrest?

May 1998

HOODWINKED by Diana Palmer

CEO Jake Edwards donned coveralls and went undercover as a mechanic to find the saboteur in his company. Nothing— or no one—would distract him, not even beautiful secretary Maureen Harris. Jake had to catch the thief—*and* the woman who'd stolen his heart!

June 1998

DEFYING GRAVITY by Rachel Lee

Tim O'Shaughnessy and his business partner, Liz Pennington, had always been close—but never *this* close. As the danger of their assignment escalated, so did their passion. When the job was over, could they ever go back to business as usual?

MEN AT WORK™

Available at your favorite retail outlet!

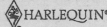 

Look us up on-line at: http://www.romance.net   PMAW1

Take 4 bestselling love stories FREE

Plus get a FREE surprise gift!

Special Limited-time Offer

Mail to Harlequin Reader Service®

3010 Walden Avenue
P.O. Box 1867
Buffalo, N.Y. 14240-1867

YES! Please send me 4 free Harlequin Presents® novels and my free surprise gift. Then send me 6 brand-new novels every month, which I will receive months before they appear in bookstores. Bill me at the low price of $3.12 each plus 25¢ delivery and applicable sales tax, if any*. That's the complete price and a savings of over 10% off the cover prices—quite a bargain! I understand that accepting the books and gift places me under no obligation ever to buy any books. I can always return a shipment and cancel at any time. Even if I never buy another book from Harlequin, the 4 free books and the surprise gift are mine to keep forever.

106 HEN CE65

Name	(PLEASE PRINT)	
Address	Apt. No.	
City	State	Zip

This offer is limited to one order per household and not valid to present Harlequin Presents® subscribers. *Terms and prices are subject to change without notice. Sales tax applicable in N.Y.

HARLEQUIN ULTIMATE GUIDES™

A series of how-to books for today's woman.

Act now to order some of these extremely
helpful guides just for you!

*Whatever the situation, Harlequin Ultimate Guides™
has all the answers!*

#80507	HOW TO TALK TO A	$4.99 U.S. ☐	
	NAKED MAN	$5.50 CAN.☐	
#80508	I CAN FIX THAT	$5.99 U.S. ☐	
		$6.99 CAN.☐	
#80510	WHAT YOUR TRAVEL AGENT	$5.99 U.S. ☐	
	KNOWS THAT YOU DON'T	$6.99 CAN.☐	
#80511	RISING TO THE OCCASION		
	More Than Manners: Real Life	$5.99 U.S. ☐	
	Etiquette for Today's Woman	$6.99 CAN.☐	
#80513	WHAT GREAT CHEFS	$5.99 U.S. ☐	
	KNOW THAT YOU DON'T	$6.99 CAN.☐	
#80514	WHAT SAVVY INVESTORS	$5.99 U.S. ☐	
	KNOW THAT YOU DON'T	$6.99 CAN.☐	
#80509	GET WHAT YOU WANT OUT OF	$5.99 U.S. ☐	
	LIFE—AND KEEP IT!	$6.99 CAN.☐	

(quantities may be limited on some titles)

TOTAL AMOUNT	$
POSTAGE & HANDLING	$
($1.00 for one book, 50¢ for each additional)	
APPLICABLE TAXES*	$ _____
TOTAL PAYABLE	$ _____
(check or money order—please do not send cash)	

To order, complete this form and send it, along with a check or money
order for the total above, payable to Harlequin Ultimate Guides, to:
In the U.S.: 3010 Walden Avenue, P.O. Box 9047, Buffalo, NY
14269-9047; **In Canada:** P.O. Box 613, Fort Erie, Ontario, L2A 5X3.

Name: _____

Address: _____ City: _____

State/Prov.: _____ Zip/Postal Code: _____

*New York residents remit applicable sales taxes.
Canadian residents remit applicable GST and provincial taxes.

◆HARLEQUIN®

Look us up on-line at: http://www.romance.net   HNFBL4

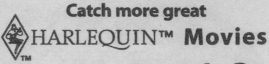

 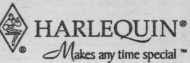

Presents Extravaganza
25 YEARS!

**With the purchase of two Harlequin Presents®
books, you can send in for a FREE Silvertone Book
Pendant. Retail value $19.95. It's our gift to you!**

FREE SILVERTONE BOOK PENDANT

On the official proof-of-purchase coupon below, fill in your name,
address and zip or postal code, and send it, plus $1.50 U.S./
$2.50 CAN. for postage and handling, (check or money order—please
do not send cash), to Harlequin books: In the U.S.: 3010 Walden
Avenue, P.O. Box 9077, Buffalo, N.Y. 14269-9077; In Canada: P.O. Box
609, Fort Erie, Ontario L2A 5X3. Please allow 4-6 weeks for delivery.
Order your Silvertone Book Pendant now! Quantities are limited. Offer
for the FREE Silvertone Book Pendant expires December 31, 1998.

Coming Next Month

HARLEQUIN PRESENTS®

THE BEST HAS JUST GOTTEN BETTER!

#1965 FANTASY FOR TWO Penny Jordan
Mollie Barnes and Alex Villiers seemed to have nothing in common. So why had she confessed her secret fantasy to him? And why was it they couldn't seem to keep away from each other?

#1966 THE DIAMOND BRIDE Carole Mortimer
(Nanny Wanted!)
Annie adored being Jessica Diamond's nanny, but her relationship with Jessica's father was complicated! Rufus had the power to make her laugh and cry—he also wanted to make love to her! But Jessica had to come first....

#1967 RENDEZVOUS WITH REVENGE Miranda Lee
When Abby's boss, Ethan Grant, asked her to pose as his lover at the conference, she knew that to him she was probably just an expensive plaything. In fact, she turned out to be a pawn in his game of revenge!

#1968 THE GROOM SAID MAYBE! Sandra Marton
(The Wedding of the Year)
It all began when Stephanie and David were seated next to each other at a wedding. Stephanie needed a lawyer, and David was one of the best, so she told him she needed money. Then David confessed he needed a fiancée....

#1969 LONG-DISTANCE MARRIAGE Sharon Kendrick
Alessandra and Cameron married in haste, believing that they could combine two careers in two different cities. But with the pressure came problems, particularly when he suggested that she leave work to have his baby....

#1970 LOVERS' LIES Daphne Clair
Joshua didn't recognize Felicia, but his obvious attraction to her gave her the means to exact revenge for his betrayal of her stepsister years ago. The problem was, Felicia herself was not immune to his charms....